MURDER FIRST GLASS

By

RON ELLIS

(A D.C.I. Glass crime novel)

First published in Great Britain in 1980 by
Robert Hale Limited
Clerkenwell House
Clerkenwell Green
London EC1R 0HT

This edition first published in 2007 by
Nirvana Books
Mayfiield Court Victoria Road
Freshfield Liverpool L37 7JL

A catalogue record for this book is available
From the British Library.

10 9 8 7 6 5 4 3 2 1

ISBN 978-09549427-4-8

Printed and bound by
Beacon DM
Unit 2 Valley Road Business Park
Gas Works Road Keighley BD21 4LY

MURDER FIRST GLASS

The Executioner is a new type of criminal. In a letter to *The Times* he announces his intention of personally restoring the death penalty in England and, within a week, his first victim is swinging at the end of a rope. Hardened criminals shiver in their cells wondering who will be next.

Meanwhile, Detective Chief Inspector Glass of Scotland Yard is racing round the country (seaside discos in Blackpool, the black ghettos of Liverpool and the once peaceful Carlisle) trying to solve the Post Office Robberies case.

Will he find the robbers before The Executioner gets to them as the trail centres on a crowded Bank Holiday football match in London.

A detective story in the best traditions of Edgar Wallace (i.e. excitement and melodrama) combined with Ron Ellis's special brand of dry humour.

We look forward to Murder *Second* Glass.

ONE

The letter to *The Times* was short and explicit.

Dear Sir,
    During the last decade there has been an alarming rise in the number of crimes of violence committed in Britain.
    I would directly attribute this to the abolition of capital punishment.
    It is a well known fact that the majority of people in this country would welcome the return of hanging, but successive governments have chosen to ignore the wishes of the electorate.
    I am therefore taking it upon myself to correct this situation by personally administering the death penalty in cases that I deem suitable.
    My first victim will die before the end of the week.

                I remain Sir,
                Yours truly,
                THE EXECUTIONER

The Editor published the letter and at the same time sent the original to Scotland Yard where it was received with mixed reactions.
    "Typewritten on Croxley Script," observed Detective Chief Inspector Knox who was placed in charge of the

investigation. " Obtainable at any stationers. Do you think it is a hoax?"

" I don't know, but I think it is a bloody good idea," said Detective Chief Inspector Glass who regretted the passing of the rack.

The Assistant Commissioner was moved to reply in an editorial the next day. He insisted that retaliatory actions by private citizens or vigilante groups could neither be tolerated nor justified and could lead to dangerous situations with private armies springing up all over the country.

" I do not expect it will have much effect on the writer of this epistle," he confided to a meeting of top level officers, " but it may deter potential imitators."

" You mean do-it-yourself enthusiasts building their own gallows at the bottom of their gardens?" asked Glass innocently.

The Assistant Commissioner chose to ignore the sarcasm. " No hope of tracing the writer, of course. Central London postmark, no prints. All we can do now is wait and hope the fellow is a harmless crank."

Meanwhile, the administration of British justice carried on as before.

TWO

Thurs., March 11th

The courtroom at the Old Bailey was hushed.

" Robert Trevellyn, you have been found guilty of wilful

murder." The judge adjusted his wig. Twenty years ago he would have worn a black cap. " For no other reason than the pleasure it afforded your warped mind, you set about this elderly defenceless man and cruelly beat him to death, regardless of his piteous cries for mercy."

The prisoner in the dock smirked, and crime reporters wrote of hardened policemen in the gallery shuddering at the youth's callous indifference.

Detective Chief Inspector Glass, who would have been unlikely to shudder at a public disembowelling, listened to the judge's words with interest.

" Christ Almighty, who does he think he is? John Betjeman?"

" Silence in court," bellowed an usher.

The judge continued. " Society must be protected from such a monster whose soul is the very embodiment of evil."

" Strong words," whispered Timothy Slade, crime reporter for *The Megaphone*. " Let us hope he backs them up with a sentence to match."

" Not a chance," snarled Glass. " Lowther is too soft. He has been swayed by all the pussy-footing do-gooders who would rather send a killer to the hospital than to the hangman."

Lord Chief Justice Lowther droned on.

" Were it not for the confidence in your deep remorse expressed by the probation officer and your psychiatrist, I should have no hesitation in sending you to prison for life."

Trevellyn continued to smirk. He was an ugly man. His face was unshaven, his drooping moustache aged him beyond his twenty years, and his hair hung in a dank, greasy lump that scarcely covered the boil on his neck. Dressed in a short-sleeved dark blue nylon shirt and black slacks, he looked well ready for the prison exercise yard. Now he stared defiantly at the bench, his grey eyes offering an overt challenge to the judge.

"As it is, I sentence you to seven years' imprisonment."

Trevellyn's smirk took on a look of triumph as he was led from the dock.

"Why not give him a bleeding medal while he's at it?" growled Glass as they filed out into the street. "No wonder the crime rate doubles and people are afraid to go out onto the streets alone at night. No wonder folk want to set themselves up as Executioners." It was the day after the letter to *The Times* and Glass was inclined to side with the writer.

"There's the old man's widow," said Slade. He pointed to a hunched figure leaning against the stone wall. Her tragic countenance contrasted vividly with that of the gloating youth in court.

Glass nodded grimly. "I was in the morgue when she identified him. Took her five minutes to be sure, he was that badly disfigured. I reckon she'll be dead within six months, nothing to live for."

"And in seven years that lad will go free."

"Five if he gets remission, and he will. He'd have to bugger the governor in his bed not to get remission these days. Colour TV in their cells, winemaking in the afternoons, requests on the Jimmy Young Show and at Christmas—" here Glass's voice broke into an interesting falsetto —"at Christmas they let the bleeders out to visit their sick mothers." The detective emitted a grunt of disgust and dug deeply into the pockets of his brown, ex-army surplus greatcoat, Lord Kitchener vintage. "If it was up to me I'd have the bastards chained to the wall and flogged. Cigarette?" He proffered a red packet of Craven A.

"No thanks, I've given them up." Timothy observed the logo curiously. "God, do they still make those things?"

8

"I believe there are one or two of us left still smoking them." Glass struggled with a match in the brisk March wind.

They walked along the front of St. Paul's. Even on this cold winter day the Cathedral steps were dotted with tourists, many of them white.

"You mentioned the Executioner before," said Timothy. "Do you think it could be for real?"

"Hard to say," said Glass. "Do you fancy a drink?"

"I should be getting back with my report."

"Rubbish. Phone it in, they won't miss you. You're not Lord Northcliffe yet, you know. Besides, *The Megaphone* doesn't go to press until nine." Glass spat a piece of loose tobacco from his mouth. It landed unnoticed on the peaked cap of a lady traffic warden. "Come on, we'll take a cab."

The detective stepped unheralded into the road, forcing an oncoming taxi to execute an impressive emergency stop.

"Yer fackin' lunatic," screamed the driver volcanically. His tone changed when he recognised his passenger. "Oh, 'allo, Mr. Glass. Didn't realise it was you, sir. Lost yer patrol car, 'ave yer?" He grinned, exposing a mouthful of inter-mittent teeth that bore passing resemblance to a vandalised graveyard.

"Couldn't afford the parking tickets, Monty. Where shall we go?" He addressed Timothy Slade.

"Why not the Wig and Pen, it is only down the road?"

"Suits me. Strand, Monty. The Wig and Pen." Glass clambered clumsily into the cab looking less like a police-man than an unsuccessful market gardener. His brown brogues were in immediate need of heels; the battered trilby covering his sparse grey hair would not have looked out of place in an Oxfam shop, and his moustache was yellowed with the accumulated residue of several million Craven A's.

9

Timothy Slade, by comparison, might well have walked out of Lord John's Carnaby Street window. His wide-lapelled, pin-striped blue suit was as currently fashionable as it had been in 1936 when Edward G. Robinson had worn an identical one in "Little Caesar". The accompanying light blue shirt toned impeccably with the silk tie, and the black patent leather shoes elevated him several inches making him, with his upswept hairstyle, almost as tall as Glass.

The taxi driver turned round as the cab stopped at the pedestrian crossing at Fetter Lane. The vehicle's lights were already illuminated as an early mist drifted in from the nearby river to darken further the grey sky.

"I 'ear that fellow Trevellyn only got seven years. Bloody scandal if you arsk me. 'Ed 'ave been topped in our day, eh, Mr. Glass?"

"Our day is gone, Monty, but you never know, it might come again." Glass thought it could not come soon enough. He might even apply for the post of public hangman. He took a last suck at his cigarette and threw the shredded cork tip out of the window straight into the startled face of an elderly head-scarved harlot waiting for a number thirteen bus.

She flinched stoically.

"Get 'em in the Army I say. Bit of discipline never 'urt nobody."

"Did me no harm," said Glass. "The tearaways you get today aren't frightened about two years' probation. They'd think twice if they had to face the birch."

"How did you find out about the verdict so soon?" enquired Timothy. "We've only just come from there ourselves."

The old driver smiled as he edged his cab forward. "You 'ear a lot in this job, don't you, Mr. Glass. Why, during the war, us cabbies knew more of what was goin' on than the 'Ome Guard and the War Office put together."

"And Scotland Yard sometimes," added the Inspector wryly.

"Never mind, Mr. Glass. With a bit of luck this Executioner bloke will settle for Trevellyn. I don't suppose there is any trace of him yet?"

"Give us a chance, Monty. The letter was only published yesterday. Anyway, I was hoping you'd be able to tell me something."

Glass relied heavily on men like the cab driver for information. Cynics at Scotland Yard had been known to comment that if all Glass's informants had been put on the regular payroll, the staff would have trebled overnight. He knew more undesirable people than anyone on the force.

"Nothing from any of the usual boys, Mr. Glass. I can't see it being any of the regular crowd myself. Most of the lads are a bit jumpy themselves. I mean, you know where you are with the Old Bill, if you'll pardon me for saying so, sir."

"Well, if you hear anything, Monty . . ." And Glass knew that it was not without the bounds of possibility that he might. Many secrets had floated audibly through the glass partitions of London taxicabs, often to the later regret of their confiders.

"Of course, Mr. Glass. Well, here we are, gents, the Wig and Pen; safe and sound."

Glass thrust a pound note through the taxi window. "Have a drink with the boys on me."

"Yer a gent, Mr. Glass. God bless yer, sir."

"Generous today aren't we," remarked Timothy as they entered the crowded vestibule of the club.

"Never does any harm to make friends." Glass waved away the offer of a coat hanger. "What are you having?"

"You'd better let me get them," said Timothy. "You have to be a member to buy drinks."

"I am a member," said Glass haughtily, "of every club that is registered in this city and of many that are not." He acknowledged a nod from the pin-striped assistant manager and walked through to the right-hand bar.

"Hello there, Mr. Glass. Haven't seen you for a while then." A professional smile accompanied the Irish brogue of the blue-coated barman. "Will it be your usual you'll be having?"

Glass nodded and turned smugly to his companion. He raised his eyebrows questioningly.

"Scotch for me."

"Coming up right away." The barman hurried about his task with birdlike movements, which reminded Timothy of a clockwork sparrow. "There we are for you. That'll be eighty pence and I'll let you put in your own lemonade."

Another pound left the Inspector's pocket.

"Oh, ta very much. Keeping well are you, Mr. Glass?"

"Can't grumble, Tristram. They haven't managed to pension me off yet." He raised his glass in the direction of the oil painting hanging over the bar. It featured a bewigged gentleman peering down with a rather pained expression. "To the judge."

"Ah yes," said Timothy. "The hanging judge."

"Judge Jeffreys. By Christ, we could do with him today and no mistake." He emptied half the Southern Comfort down his throat at the first attempt. "Let's go and sit down."

He led the way to the narrow black seat that circumscribed the stained glass windows, a seat barely wide enough to contain his considerable bulk, and squeezed alongside a gilt and onyx standard lamp. The red shade of the lamp toned tastefully with the gold velvet curtains that framed the window.

"Right," said the detective. "Now tell me what you've heard about The Executioner."

"I thought I asked you that."

"Yes, but I don't know anything. I'm only the police. I thought that you, as Fleet Street's leading crime reporter . . ." Glass coughed expectantly.

"Yes, well all London is talking about it but nobody actually knows anything. The letter just appeared from nowhere."

"How about one of these political activist groups?"

"There has been no follow up yet. Here, give me your glass and I'll get them in. Same again is it?" Without waiting for an answer, Timothy walked over to the bar.

Glass cast his glance round the room. The walls of the club were filled with framed journalistic paraphernalia of the ages; facsimiles of famous front pages, photographs, engravings and the passenger list of the *Queen Mary*'s Trial Trip in 1936.

He sighed. In a couple of hours he would be off duty. Thursday was his Old Tyme Dancing Night at the Compton Road Welfare and Social Club. He consulted his ex-Navy Chronograph which, for twenty-two pounds, guaranteed to tell him the time in six major world capitals underwater. "Four o'clock," he murmured to nobody in particular.

It was a significant time. At four o'clock precisely occurred the Leyton Post Office Robbery.

THREE

P.C. Michael Spencer manoeuvred his Panda car along the congested Leyton High Road towards Walthamstow. It was late afternoon and the pavements were packed with afternoon shoppers regurgitated from the crowded super-markets. Screaming children with chocolate-stained faces sat in their push-chairs like charioteers locked in combat as their mothers fought for empty spaces without spilling off the kerb.

When he was eight and a half Michael Spencer had read Enid Blyton's *Mystery of the Spiteful Letters* from cover to cover and decided he wanted to be a detective like Fatty of the Find-Outers. His ambition had never wavered. His career to date in the Force had been un-eventful—the usual round of drunks, baby batterers, wife beaters, straying animals, errant motorists, part-time pros-titutes, infant burglars and misunderstood shoplifters—but now that he had been put on the Pandas he looked forward to the challenge of dealing with real crime. He was still only twenty-three. His uniform was well pressed, his black shoes shone and his buttons glistened. He would have preferred more pay, but his ideals came first and he would never have dreamt of coming out on strike. He was proud of being a policeman.

The traffic stopped at a zebra crossing. Michael Spencer sat back and imagined he was on his way to the West End to deal with a bomb scare at Oxford Circus tube station.

He would successfully defuse the bomb just in time for Harold Wilson to alight from the 3.55 from Marble Arch and offer him the George Cross.

"Bravo Two, come in please."

The radio cut into his thoughts. He picked up the receiver.

"Bravo Two, go ahead."

"Bravo Two, proceed to Leyton Road Post Office. Attempted robbery."

Adrenalin raced through Michael's veins. He switched on his siren and blue flashing light and edged out of the traffic line.

"Bravo Two, on my way. Roger."

This was the chance he had been waiting for. He steered the car down the centre of the road, driving as fast as he dare, causing other vehicles to pull into the kerb. Now was the moment for him to prove himself.

Nobody had mentioned that the robbers were armed.

The two-mile journey took him three minutes. He pulled up outside the Post Office, tyres squealing dramatically.

He could not have timed it better. Or worse.

As he leapt out of the car he was immediately confronted by two men emerging from the doorway. One had black curly hair around his ears and the other was blond with thick fingers.

He noticed the fingers particularly because they were holding the gun.

Both men wore masks, children's masks that were made grotesque by these circumstances. He recognised one of them as Yogi Bear.

"Get back, copper." The muffled voice from behind the blond man's mask meant business. The other man dragged a mailbag to a rusting Ford Executive parked in front of the police Panda car. Shoppers around had scattered, some peeping from doorways along the street to see what was happening. Somewhere a woman screamed "Fetch help," but Michael Spencer was the only help there was.

The black-haired man shoved the mailbag onto the back seat and started the Executive's engine. His colleague edged his way to join him, still training the gun on the young policeman.

Michael Spencer's mouth was dry. His heart pounded and his legs seemed to be attached to a ball and chain. Should he run back to the car and radio for help? No, there would not be time. Besides, he might never make it. The car was three or four yards behind him and they might shoot him in the back. He would have to face them. And now. The second man had nearly reached the Executive. Michael remembered to look at the registration number: JCY313. He had to stop it leaving. The people were waiting for him to act. He, Police Constable 3647, was the sole representative of the law. No Chief Constable or Superintendent to shield behind. It was all up to him.

He also knew that if he captured these men it could mean promotion. Certainly a recommendation. For a second he could hear in his mind the accolades he would receive at the Police Ball he was attending that very night. "Well done, Spencer. A brave arrest." But then came another voice, his own, like an echo across a canyon.

"Give me that gun." He took a step forward. He knew it was safe. Had not Clint Eastwood done the same thing a hundred times on television? Faced with the decision they never shot you.

Then a loud bang. A stab of pain seared through his head and from a long way off he heard screams. Then the roar of a car engine. Then quiet.

16

He could not think why he was lying on this cold stone pavement or why this liquid running down his face was so warm. In his mind he could see a tiny face that looked like his baby daughter and he tried to call to her, but some of the liquid ran down his throat and made him choke. He coughed to clear it, but it hurt him to cough, and more of the liquid ran down. And then the pain in his head started to get worse and he felt like his brain was going to burst. He screamed, but nothing came out. He choked again and felt his mind going blank, then suddenly the pain stopped, he felt himself going to sleep and nothing mattered any more.

The watch on his wrist ticked on. One second past four.

P.C. Michael Spencer, carrying out his duty defending society against its enemies, had drowned to death in his own blood.

The ranks of the British Constabulary were reduced by one.

The bungalows on the new Woodtree Estate were identical. Little bigger than garages, they were individually distinguishable only by the colour of their paintwork, the variety of trees in their gardens and the eccentricity of ornaments in the lounge bay windows.

Number 27 Laburnum Close boasted yellow climbing roses, a laburnum tree, primrose woodwork, primrose guttering and a purple front door. In the Georgian front window was displayed an imitation china vase shaped like a porpoise with a yellow rose between its lips.

The streets on the estate bore names to recall the pleasant country fields that the builders had destroyed. Low Stiles, Far Meadow, Hawthorn Way and Willow Walk. Here and there an odd oak tree had been left standing to give the illusion to those people who had never seen a cow alive that they really were in the country.

A convoy of young mothers straggled along the network of avenues, some wheeling prams with shopping piled underneath and babies tucked up inside. Small children, out of afternoon school, rode alongside on an assortment of pedal machines, satchels hanging from the handlebars. Older children travelled precariously by skateboard, surfing down the sidewalks, and some kicked footballs and pretended they were Kevin Keegan. An electric bakery van chugged from door to door making the last of the day's deliveries, and a converted ambulance filled with groceries stood at the end of the lane, a substitute for the corner shop the planners had neglected to build. A paper boy, on a rusty bicycle, whistled in competition with the dusk chorus of starlings overhead.

Inside the modern pinewood kitchen of Number 27 Laburnum Close a young housewife was preparing dinner. Her name was Carol. A transistor radio perched on the stainless steel drainer played the same pop record that was being heard in a million similar households all over the country.

" Can I roll the pastry, Mummy?" A small girl with ash-blonde curls reached eagerly for the rolling-pin. Carol smiled and handed it to her. She had to stand on tiptoe to reach the baking surface. This was Fiona and she was three and a half.

" What time is Daddy home today, Mummy?"

" Half-past six, darling." Half-past six, and at nine they were going to the Annual Dance, which meant that she had not got much time to finish the dinner, take a bath and arrange her evening clothes. She wanted to make a good impression in front of her husband's bosses. She knew how important the right wife could be.

"No, Fiona. Don't give that pastry to Haggis. You'll make him sick."

Carol removed a wad of half-chewed pastry from the mouth of a moulting Yorkshire terrier and threw it in the pedal bin before continuing with the preparation of the meal.

She filled a casserole dish with vegetables, mushrooms, celery and potatoes, added cubes of pre-cooked steak and pressed the rolled-out pastry firmly over the top of the dish. Setting the regulo at four, she put the dish into the gas oven and set the timer for six-thirty.

"What time are Grandpa and Nana coming?"

"They'll be here for dinner, pet, and then they'll stay with you while Daddy and I go out."

"Where are you going?"

"Just to a dance." Carol finished washing the dishes, wiped her hands and took off her plastic apron. "Now you go in the lounge and watch television while Mummy gets ready, Fiona. Playschool will be on soon."

She went across to the bathroom to run the bathwater, taking the transistor with her to stand on the closed lid of the toilet. She undressed in the bedroom and padded naked across the fitted hall carpet, looking less than her twenty-two years with her small breasts and trim figure. As she slid beneath the steaming pine-scented bubbles into the bath, the voice of Tony Blackburn on Radio One announced that it was one minute to four o'clock.

Sixty seconds later, Carol Spencer, policeman's wife, became a widow.

By the time a second Panda car arrived at the Leyton Road Post office, the Executive was long gone and Michael

Spencer had been dead for four minutes.

Within seconds messages were flashed to police stations and patrols cars throughout the city. Every policeman in London was alerted. Off-duty men stayed on, giving up their time to help find the men who had brutally killed one of their colleagues.

At Scotland Yard, the Assistant Commissioner was in conference when the information was relayed to him. He did not hesitate.

"We are taking over the enquiry," he told a messenger. He pressed a button on his intercom. "Send for Detective Chief Inspector Glass."

FOUR

Detective Chief Inspector Glass was putting his second Southern Comfort to his lips when the call to duty came in the form of a bleeping sound emanating from the folds of his ex-army greatcoat.

"It's like being on the bloody lifeboats," he grumbled, "always on bloody call. I blame Marconi." He fumbled beneath his coat and produced a pocket radio from the pockets of his serge suit. "Glass," he snarled into it.

"The A.C. for you, just a minute."

"Glass?"

"Yes, sir." The detective listened to the crackling voice and his face hardened. "I'll be right there, sir." He pressed a button on the radio. "Operations? Send my car to the Wig and Pen in the Strand and I want Sergeant Moon with it."

"Trouble?" The newshound in Timothy Slade spoke out.

"Young bobby shot in Leyton."

"Badly hurt?"

"Dead."

"What happened?"

"A Post Office raid. He tried to stop them."

"Single handed?"

"So it seems."

"What about passers-by?"

"Oh, come on, Tim. You surely don't expect the public to help. Christ, these days they'd tread on a blind man to be first in a bus queue. It's a wonder they didn't open the car door to help the villains get away." He wiped his nose with the end of his knuckle. "Probably thought it was the BBC shooting Z-Cars."

"So the men got away?"

"In a big car according to two dozen eye witnesses."

"Did they take much?"

"About five hundred pounds and the day's mail, that's all. Hardly enough to justify some bugger's life."

"So what are the chances of catching them?"

"We'll catch the bastards, Tim, make no mistake. With a bobby killed we'll catch them. Come on, let's go outside and wait for the car. I could do with some fresh air. Just before I come off duty too." This meant goodbye to his evening at the Compton Road Welfare and Social Club. He had been looking forward to his old time dancing, and particularly to the attentions of Mrs. Lewthwaite, a widowed lady of his acquaintance who often accompanied him in the slow foxtrot. This gave him another reason to hate the villains. Carol Spencer would find nobody more determined to track down her husband's killers.

"Any chance of a lift down there?" asked Timothy Slade as they emerged into the chilly darkness of the Strand.

"Why not?" allowed the Inspector. "Although you'd probably be quicker by bus."

But they had only a few minutes to wait for the car. An unmarked Cortina pulled up beside the kerb and the driver jumped out, saluted Glass and opened the back door for the two men to climb inside. In the front passenger seat sat Detective Sergeant Moon.

"Can't have a quiet drink in peace," grumbled Glass by way of greeting. "You know Timothy Slade, don't you?"

Moon did not, but he gave a nod that could have been interpreted as a gesture of acquiescence or a greeting. Slade nodded back.

"Come on, lad," Glass addressed the driver. "Step on it. Let's try to get there before the TV cameras this time. We don't want the whole nation glued to their television sets waiting for our arrival on the Six o'clock News."

The young driver twitched nervously. He did not look old enough to have grown the moustache that sprouted delicately on his upper lip. Glass idly wondered if it was stuck on."

"Know all about this, do you, lad?"

"Vaguely, sir."

"Vaguely? That's no way for a policeman to know anything. Vaguely!"

"No, sir." He executed a neat U-turn towards Fleet Street.

"Bad business this shooting," interrupted Sergeant Moon hastily.

"What annoys me," said Glass, "is that the bastard

22

who shot him will end up no worse off than if he had just robbed the Post Office. Murder ranks no higher than armed robbery these days. It costs no more to kill."

Timothy Slade agreed. "You are quite right. Look at Trevellyn this afternoon. Seven years for beating an old man to death."

"They'd have laughed at you if you had told that to anyone in the Force in the old days." Glass opened a new packet of Craven A, unwrapping the silver paper with the dedication of a chiropodist peeling a difficult corn.

"There is only one way to treat violence," said Timothy Slade vehemently, "And that is with more violence. It is the only language the villains understand. They aren't afraid of the law any more. It is too soft."

"Well, that is the fault of the magistrates and the do-gooders," growled Glass, "not the police."

The Cortina reached the top of Ludgate Hill.

"It is only fear, you know, that keeps people law abiding. Moses knew that when he invented the Ten Commandments. Disobey me and you shall be cast into Hellfire. That kept the Israelites quiet."

On the front seat, Sergeant Moon plucked at the small hairs on his fingers and said nothing. After working with Glass for ten months he was used to these oratories. He often wondered if the Inspector was preparing for a career in Parliament when he retired from the Force, and made a mental note to check out Hyde Park Corner one Sunday afternoon.

"So what you will get," continued Glass, "is people starting to take the law into their own hands. Like The Executioner."

"You are taking it seriously at the Yard then?"

"We have to until we know otherwise."

" But you must receive thousands of crank letters yourselves. I know we do at *The Megaphone*."

Glass smiled. " Yes, I notice he did not send the letter to your paper."

" The fellow is obviously a snob."

" I wonder who he will pick for his first victim," said Moon, who felt he ought to say something.

" How about Trevellyn? An obvious choice I would have thought."

" Too recent, Tim. If this bloke is for real, I reckon he already has his first victim lined up. And who is to say he will only go after murderers? A couple of football hooligans swinging from a gibbet outside Old Trafford on a Saturday afternoon might not be a bad idea."

" I take it I can print that," smiled Timothy.

" I'll deny it and sue you for libel before the print is dry. Christ, here we are at last."

The scene at Leyton High Road resembled an extravagant film set. Floodlights had been set up around the Post Office and a sizable crowd of onlookers were cordoned off from the spot where Michael Spencer's body still lay. Traffic was being diverted through side streets, motorcycle patrolmen with walkie talkie sets directing operations. All around, uniformed policemen were running about as if in a silent newsreel. Glass almost expected to be shown to a deckchair with his name printed on the back.

" Shot in the face at close range," announced the Police Surgeon who had just completed his examination when Glass arrived. " The lad didn't stand a chance."

He lifted the sheet for the Inspector to see the dead officer's face.

" Christ, he's just a kid," said Glass sadly. " Any family?"

" A wife and a little girl I believe."

Glass felt sick with rage. Two people's lives ruined for a start. Repercussions that would last for ever. And there would be more.

"Anybody see the actual killing?"

The driver of the second Panda car spoke up. "If you mean witnesses, sir, we've hundreds of them with a hundred descriptions to match." His exaggeration was caused by bitterness, and Glass saw no reason to contest the point. "Six people claim to have seen the shot. They are inside the Post Office now." He pointed to the throng on the perimeter of the disaster. "And half that lot say they saw the car."

"I know, a big one."

The constable smiled, recognising in his superior a frustration similar to his own.

"Excuse me, Chief Inspector." A gangling man in a tweed suit of indeterminate colour tapped Glass on the shoulder. "My name is Whelk, Detective Inspector Whelk. I have been in charge of this enquiry," he looked sharply at the other, "so far."

"Really?" said Glass. "Well, I shall want to interview the six eye witnesses and the postmaster."

The Police Surgeon stepped forward. "Nothing more I can do here. The pathologist and the forensic boys are on their way. I've got patients of my own to see."

"Any ideas, George?"

"At a guess, I'd say it was an A32 bullet. Probably from a Walther."

"Which is like saying the car was a Ford."

"I believe it was," said the surgeon.

A uniformed constable drove the dead man's Panda car back to the station.

"Right," said Glass. "What are we waiting for? Let's

have a look at these witnesses."

He led the way into the little shop. It was gloomy inside, dimly lit with mahogany fittings and brown lino. A modern illuminated greetings card rack, which lined the left-hand wall, stood out like the showpiece at Blackpool illuminations. In the centre of the floor was a revolving stand of men's glossy magazines containing photographs of naked ladies more suited to a gynaecology manual. More respectable periodicals were displayed along the right-hand side together with a selection of sweets and chocolates. The Post Office section was contained in a sombre alcove at the back of the shop. Three pairs of scales at the front of the counter hid a collection of forms, licences and money orders, whilst up on the wall, a collage of peeling posters offered a wealth of advice and instruction from Her Majesty's Government. One advocated the advisability of making long-distance phone calls in the middle of the night to save money, and another told of good tidings for pensioners which would be revealed upon request at the counter. Glass thought he might ask for a leaflet later.

Behind the wire grill the elderly postmistress sat trembling on a wooden chair. Her husband brought in a mug of tea.

"Drink this, Elsie. I've put a drop of whisky in it," he explained to the Inspector.

Glass nodded. He approved of anything with whisky in it.

"Mr. and Mrs. Lucas," announced Whelk. "This is Detective Chief Inspector Glass. From Scotland Yard," he added, venomously.

"We've been terrified something like this would happen one day," confided the old man to Glass. "It stands to reason. Banks are getting too difficult to rob with all their alarm systems and security guards. A post office is easy.

26

Maybe not so much money, but easy. What sort of defence are we, me and Elsie?"

The old lady spoke up. "Alec shouldn't have to fight them. Not with his back."

"Nobody asked him to fight them, Mrs. Lucas."

"He has to wear a truss, you know."

"Especially a man with a gun."

"Shoved it straight through the grill he did. Right into my face. I thought me end had come. Then the other bloke came round the counter and helped himself to the money out of the drawer."

"How much was there?"

"About six hundred pounds altogether I would say."

"Cash?"

"And money orders and postal orders. And they took the mailbags too."

"No customers in the shop at the time?"

"No, they chose their time well. But when they were round the counter taking the money from the drawer, someone came in, saw the men's masks and ran out again. It must have been them what gave the alarm."

"We received a 999 call at 15.54," interjected the local inspector.

"They made us open the safe, but there was nothing in it except a few savings certificates."

Glass walked round the counter to examine the safe. Two men from the Forensic Lab. had arrived and were kneeling on the floor sprinkling powder onto everything.

"Praying for guidance," observed Glass whimsically to Moon, who was following. They passed on to the till.

"These witnesses . . ."

"In the back," interjected Whelk.

"And no definite descriptions you say?"

27

"They had masks on," interrupted Mrs. Lucas. "Children's masks."

"We know one was blond and the other was stocky," pressed Whelk, anxious that Scotland Yard should be aware of every observation his division had made, "with black hair."

"One was Yogi Bear," said Mrs. Lucas.

"Pardon."

"From the television. Yogi Bear."

"We think the other may have been Barney Flintstone but we can't be sure." Whelk averted his eyes from the malicious glare of the Scotland Yard man. "He was one with the black hair."

"What about the car? Big, I believe?"

"More than that." Inspector Whelk preened himself at his extra knowledge. His military moustache, modelled on the one worn by Errol Flynn in his role as General Custer, twitched proudly. "It was definitely a Ford."

"That must narrow it down to a few million."

"Possibly a Grenada or a Cortina, but we think it was old so it may have been a Zephyr."

"No registration number?"

"No." The Errol Flynn moustache drooped a little. A dewdrop formed in the nostrils above it. Glass watched it, fascinated.

"Bound to be stolen, anyway. It will turn up by morning no doubt." He turned to the Forensic men, still kneeling like Buddhists at the shrine. "No prints anywhere I suppose?"

One of the men looked up from his dusting. "Nothing so far. Its odds on they wore gloves."

"Surprise, surprise. Well, I suppose I'd better see these witnesses." He turned to Sergeant Moon. "Got your notebook and pencil?"

"Do you need me any more?" asked Whelk.

"Have you got someone running round the joke-shops of London to find out who bought those masks?"

Whelk's moustache turned to walrus as he realised that the thought had not occurred to him. But he would not admit it. "I thought I'd leave that to you, Chief Insector."

Glass uttered a cough of disbelief and was pleased to see the dewdrop finally trickle down Whelk's moustache into his waiting mouth.

"You see to it, Moon. And have someone drive Mr. and Mrs. Lucas to the Yard to look at a few photographs."

"But we didn't see their faces," reminded Mrs. Lucas nervously.

Glass ignored her. "And I want to know which of our Top Twenty armed robbers are out of jail at the moment."

"What about my notebook, sir? You told me to get my notebook."

Glass sighed impatiently. "Oh yes; all right. The constable here can drive them to the Yard." He indicated their driver.

"—er one thing." Detective Inspector Whelk opened his mouth.

"What is it?"

"The dead man. Nobody has told his missus yet."

"Well, that's your job. You knew him, didn't you?"

"Not really. You see, he'd just been transferred to our division. I thought if someone from the Yard could go it might help a bit. Let the lady know something is being done if you follow me."

"All right. I'll go myself later. All the dirty jobs," he grumbled to Moon.

Timothy Slade appeared from nowhere. "Can I come

along to see her? Human interest story."

"Christ, you lot are like vultures, but yes, because I want you to do something for me. I want this little lot on the front page tomorrow, pregnant pop stars and economic crises permitting of course. I want everybody in the country looking out for old Fords. Five hundred pounds is not much money and this Post Office will only be the first. I want to catch these buggers before the second, before more people are killed. Besides, if we don't catch them, someone else might, though I don't know that that would not be a bad idea."

Timothy Slade smiled. He knew exactly to whom the detective referred.

Glass turned to the postmistress. "Have you got a back room, Mrs. Lucas, that I can use to interview the witnesses?"

She exchanged glances with her husband. "There's the parlour you could go in. You'd be private in there. Through that door behind you."

FIVE

The back parlour was dark like the shop, the only window facing East and being overlooked by a factory. The 75-watt bulb hidden by an old glass lampshade did not help; neither did the dark brown paintwork and beige floral wallpaper. A Cannon Gas Miser, burning in the tiled fireplace, contributed to the stuffy atmosphere in the small room.

The furniture was Edwardian; a two-seater couch and

pair of winged armchairs, all covered in floral chintz; a faded Axminster carpet, in dull beige to match the wallpaper; and, dominating the room, a gargantuan walnut sideboard. Two framed photographs depicting wedding groups stood at either end of its vast top like sentries. In the middle, next to a blunt cactus, a cut-glass vase overflowed with household paraphernalia—loose Green Shield stamps, a pair of nail clippers, elastic bands, a shoehorn, miscellaneous receipts and bills, a 1971 theatre programme and a copy of *Old Moore's Almanack* for 1975.

Behind the vase was a gold-framed photograph of a young man with Brylcreemed hair in an RAF uniform. Glass guessed that this must be the Lucas's son and wondered if he had survived his picture. The old lady caught his gaze.

"Our son Gerald, Inspector. He was killed in the War."

"Oh, I'm sorry."

"We had no other children. Gerald was the only one. He was just twenty-three when he died." The same age as Michael Spencer. "Anyway, you don't want to hear our troubles. Will it be all right for you in here?"

"Oh yes. You go off with the constable. We'll be fine."

Sergeant Moon escorted them out, then returned to the Inspector.

"They're all waiting in the parcels room."

"Who are?"

"The eye-witnesses."

Glass snorted. Eye witnesses! Well, I suppose we'd better see them, much good that it will do."

"You don't hold out much hope then?"

"Do you? From my experience, half of them will be here to find out from us what's going on and the rest will just have come for the excitement. No, we won't find the villains

31

this way, but we will have to talk to them just in case. I may be wrong I suppose."

His tone suggested he did not think it likely, and Moon hurriedly ushered in a spindly man of fifty wearing a grey overcoat, white muffler and cloth cap. The Inspector walked across to him, beaming.

" Mr. Onsloe, isn't it? Do take a seat Mr. Onsloe. He showed the man to the large oak dining-table by the window and pulled out a chair for him. Glass took the one opposite.

" Now then, Mr. Onsloe. That's a good Northern name, isn't it?" Glass liked to establish early friendly relations.

" Aye. I come from Thirsk in Yorkshire."

" I know it well. Hotel called the Golden Fleece in the Market Square."

" Aye, that's it."

" They haven't knocked it down yet then?" Glass smiled expansively and took a suck at his cigarette. " I'm sorry. Do you smoke, Mr. Onsloe?"

" Only my pipe."

" Well, feel free." Glass felt that a few clouds of burning Condor Sliced could do little damage to the Lucas's already brown walls.

" Now then, tell me in your own words what you saw this afternoon."

" Well, I saw them shoot 't bobby."

" Both of them?"

" Nay lad, just the one. 'T other were in 't car ready for off."

" And the one who shot him; what did he look like?"

" Not as big as thee. He wore this silly mask, a bear I think it were. The bobby walked up to him and held his hand out, for 't gun I suppose, and 't fellow shot him in 't face."

32

" Then what?"

" 'T bobby fell over and he were off in 't car then folks started shouting and running about before 't next bobbys came."

Glass held his breath. " I don't suppose you noticed the make of the car or the number?"

" Eh, it were a long time since I bothered my head with cars and stuff. But it were a big one and it were brown, nigger brown."

" I don't expect you'd recognise the killer again?"

" I would if he wore that mask."

" Probably he won't wear it all the time," said Glass icily.

" Happen," retorted the other. There was a silence. Glass could not think of anything else worthwhile to ask. He looked across at Moon who was still busily writing in his notebook, lips pursed in deep concentration. Glass wondered if he ought to speak more slowly in future to compensate for the sergeant's secretarial deficiencies.

" Well, Mr. Onsloe," he said, " if you remember anything else you must get in touch with me at Scotland Yard."

" Aye, if I do." He rose from the table, and Moon, his writing now finished, led him out.

The second witness was a fat, middle-aged woman with straggly hair festooning the frayed edges of her headscarf. She described herself as a housewife. She had heard a scream which had brought her running out of the launderette down the road whence she had " seen everything ".

" What sort of scream was it, Mrs. Ince?"

" How do you mean?"

" What I say. What sort of scream?"

" I dunno. A scream's a scream innit?" She revolved day-old Dentyne round her mouth.

"Was it like this? AAAAAARRRGGH!" Glass let out an ear-splitting roar seldom heard outside of buffalo country. Moon dropped his pencil and Mrs. Ince jumped out of her skin. "Well?" demanded Glass, reverting to human sounds.

"Er no, not like that. More like er—" a feeble bleat escaped her chapped lips. "Baaaaah!"

"That doesn't sound like a noise to bring you running from the clatter of your washing machine."

"I wasn't at the machines. I was at the door at the time watching for my bus."

"So you were looking down the road and saw it all happen then?"

"No, my bus comes the other way. But I turned round when I heard the scream. There was a lot of screaming started then. It was like that mass hysteria that you read about in the papers."

"So what it boils down to is that all you saw was a lot of people standing about screaming?"

"Not standing, they were running most of them."

"But no suggestion of shooting or cars being driven away at fast speeds or anything like that?"

"No, nothing like that. Is that what happened then? They say a policeman was killed. Is that right?"

"Thank you for helping us, Mrs. Ince. Moon."

The sergeant hurried to take the lady away, averting his eyes from Glass's "I Told You So" look.

The next lady was younger, in her thirties, and wearing a once white woollen coat that barely reached her knees. When she sat down she crossed her legs, revealing an unpleasant amount of bulging thigh.

"Mrs. Hargreaves, isn't it?"

"Mrs. Krinks."

"Ah." Not the best of starts. He had read the list

34

wrongly. His eyes rested speculatively on Mrs. Krinks' uppermost thigh. The blue veins showing clearly through the stretched tights reminded him of motorways on his road atlas. " Ah," he repeated. " Yes, here we are, Mrs. Isobel Krinks of Maida Vale. Can you tell me what you saw out there, Mrs. Krinks?" He waited expectantly.

" Well, I was coming out of the greengrocer's next door with my apples. I always get apples on a Wednesday because my Jack likes apple sauce with his sausages, you see, so I went to Rylands because they do a nice Bramley, and I was just coming out when I saw this police car come racing up and this copper jumped out and then these two men came out of next door with sacks." She paused at last for breath, and Glass watched in pity as Moon's pen scribbled furiously and bravely to keep up.

" One of them ran to the car and the other stood there in front of this copper; then the next thing you know there's this bang and the copper drops to the floor and the man jumps in the car with the other one and they are off."

The Inspector hurriedly got a word in. " It seems that you saw the whole incident, Mrs. Krinks. Now, this is important. Did you see either the men or their car well enough to identify them?"

" The car was green, dark green. I know because my brother-in-law George has one the same colour only his was a Hillman and this one was a Ford."

" Are you sure it was a Ford?"

" Oh yes, and a big one, not one of them Fiestas like Jack's boss's wife has got. This was like the ones they use for taxis. I should have got the number shouldn't I?"

" And the men?" asked Glass, ignoring this.

" Do you know, I couldn't see their faces because they had these masks on, children's masks. But one was big

35

and stocky like a miner and the other had long blond hair."

"Very observant Mrs. Krinks, but you'd not recognize them again?"

"Oh no." She changed legs and Glass was treated to a further section of the M6.

"Well, thank you, anyway. You've been most helpful," he lied. Three down, three to go. His good humour was fading fast, and when the fourth witness turned out to be a traffic warden he felt positively disagreeable. The previous Saturday he had been booked for parking too close to the corner of Loftus Road during Queens Park Rangers home game with Liverpool.

"Miss Grimes, isn't it?" His emphasis of the Miss suggested she had not only been passed over but trampled underfoot in the rush to the altar. Now she was on the menopausal side of forty.

"That's right." Her voice matched her short straight hair and thick arms. Above her lips was the faint trace of a moustache.

"Can you tell me anything that may be of value?"

"I saw the car. A Ford."

"The number?"

"Too far away to see. I was on the other side of the road, but it was either maroon or brown and a big one."

"You don't know the model?"

"No." Glass gazed Heavenwards for Divine Help, but none was forthcoming.

"How about the men running to the car?"

"Too far away to pick out clearly. It was almost dark you know. They were young though."

"How do you know?"

"They way they ran. Athletic sort of gait."

"I see."

"I was writing out a ticket at the time. I only really looked up when I heard the shot and the scream." She spoke defiantly.

"Right. Thank you, Miss Grimes." Two left. Just as he had thought: a waste of time. He watched the fifth person come in, another middle-aged woman, perhaps a trifle better dressed than the others. Her brown and mustard suit suggested House of Fraser rather than Walthamstow Market.

"You are . . . ?"

"Mrs. Hargreaves." Yes. The accent was very St. John's Wood.

"Oh yes, the missing Mrs. Hargreaves."

"I beg your pardon."

"Nothing. Private joke. Now then, did you see anything to help us, Mrs. Hargreaves?"

"Merely your constable get a bullet through his skull, Chief Inspector." She spoke sharply, and both policemen sat up a little straighter.

"You were close to them, were you?"

"I was about ten feet away from their car. The first man ran towards me with mailbags and things in his grasp. I almost had to stand back to allow him access to the vehicle. His friend followed, but unfortunately your policeman arrived on the scene and tried to stop him."

"Why do you say unfortunately?"

"Well, he got shot, didn't he? Had he been a minute later he would still be with us."

"Had he been a minute earlier he might have stopped the robbery."

She shrugged. "Possibly."

"Having been so close, can you describe the men at all? I know they were wearing masks," he added hastily, "but had they any distinguishing features? Boils, growths, club feet?"

"They seemed singularly fit young men to me, devoid of blemish and with a fair turn of speed considering the weight of the mailbags."

"Ah, you say young?"

"In their twenties I would say from their general carriage."

"How about the car. You were close to it."

"But with my back to it. I was too engrossed in the shooting."

"Well," said Glass, "we have your address if we need you. Thank you."

It was five-thirty. Glass thought of Mrs. Lewthwaite. He would be lucky if he saw his own bed tonight, never mind hers.

Moon's voice sounded more insistent. "This is Mr. Livesey who raised the alarm."

A florid young man with sideburns and large spectacles came to the table.

"Ah, Mr. Livesey, do sit down." This was their final hope of any clue and, looking at it, Glass was not impressed. It wore a Fair Isle jumper and shifted on its seat twining its sweating hands together and opened and shut its mouth like a simpleton. It was about nineteen.

"I believe you work in a local convenience, Mr. Livesey. In charge down there, are you?"

"Oh no, sir. Mr. Shatwell's in charge. But I hope to have a hall of my own one day." He looked wistful. "With marble urinals."

The summit of man's ambition, thought Glass. To run your own pisshouse.

"Now then," he said. "You raised the alarm I am told.

That was quick thinking, very commendable. But what exactly made you realise anything was wrong when you first entered the Post Office?"

Mr. Livesey spoke easily, almost frothing at the mouth. "This man behind the grill. He had a mask on. And the other had a gun, just like in my comics. So I ran out again."

"To the telephone?"

"There was one outside."

"Why didn't they chase you?"

"Couldn't have heard me. I have crêpe soles. I was too quick for them anyway. I opened the door, saw the gun and whoosh!—" he threw his hands over his shoulder to illustrate his alacrity, "I was in the phone box dialling 999."

"And when you came out again?"

"They were driving away."

"Took you rather a long time to telephone, didn't it?"

"I dialled 998 the first time. I was trembling a bit. I've waited all my life for something like this to happen. I've got every 'Master Detective' since February 1973. I keep them in my room with my kites."

Glass leaned forward. He spoke in the voice he used for addressing dolts. "Then as a master detective, you will have known to get the car's registration number."

The youth beamed. "Oh yes, I remembered that all right."

"Well?" Glass held his breath.

"I couldn't see it. My eyes aren't so good." He touched the pebble lenses. "It was too far away." He began to cry.

Glass rose to his feet. "That's it then. Don't worry, lad. You did very well to ring us so promptly." He let the boy make his own way out of the parlour and he looked across to the sergeant.

" Well?" he demanded.

" You were right, I suppose," conceded Moon. " But if you disregard eye witnesses what else have we to go on?"

" Information about crime," lectured Glass, " most often comes from criminals. Jealousy, revenge, money, these are more powerful motives than loyalty. We'll hear a few tales before long. The snouts will be on the phone. Then there is the car. That will turn up somewhere and maybe they will have left something behind. Or they will do another job and bungle it. Or we'll get a tip-off."

" All a bit vague, though, isn't it? I mean, we've no actual definite line of enquiry, have we?" Moon's voice tapered out nervously.

" We are doing all the obvious things, aren't we? Checking on joke shops looking for people who bought Yogi Bear masks, taking the Lucas's to look at the files, interviewing those dickheads, looking all over the country for big Ford cars. All definite lines of enquiry as you put it. I'd say we were doing very well. What I am getting at, though, privately between you and I, is that it is all a bleeding waste of time."

" Then why do we do it?"

" Well, we've got to do something, haven't we?" said Glass exasperatedly. " I mean, think of the newspapers. It would look good, wouldn't it, on the front page of *The Megaphone*, ' Scotland Yard are sitting back waiting for Eddie The Nose to ring '?"

" I see what you mean," said Moon glumly. He felt he had learnt more in his ten months with Glass than he had in his previous four years on the Force, although he was not quite sure whether or not this was to his advantage.

" Let's be off then," said the Inspector. " We've got to

go and see this poor bugger's wife." He looked at Moon's melancholy face. " Cheer up, lad. We'll get them in the end. Trust your old Inspector." He shut the parlour door behind them. " Going out tonight, were you?"

" Only to the pictures with my fiancée."

" Ah yes." Everyone had heard of Moon's fiancée, but nobody had actually met her. It was believed she was called Ethel and had religion. " She'll be used to sitting in on her own by now."

They walked out into the floodlit street. The rain was now falling heavily and a makeshift plastic tent had been erected over the body as the Pathologist completed his examination. Glass went across to him.

" Anything unusual there, Wilfred?"

The specialist glanced up. " Nothing but a bullet in the brain, if you call that unusual. He died from asphyxiation after inhaling his own blood."

" Not a pleasant way to go."

" Better than cancer I would think."

" Not at 23," said Glass. " He'd not even had time to join the Rotary Club."

" Anyway, I've done all I can here now. Can I have the body moved to the public mortuary for the post mortem?"

" If David Bailey there has finished." He pointed to the photographer snapping away from different angles.

" I'm done now," said 'David Bailey' whose name was Roberts. " I'll come up with you to the mortuary."

" I'll be along myself later with his wife. She'll have to identify him." He found Inspector Whelk and ordered him to stay at the scene of the crime in charge of everything and sent the ambulance to transport the body of Michael Spencer for dissection. "That's about it then here," he said to Moon. " Have we got the woman's address?" Moon handed him a slip of paper. " Right, let's go." They walked over to the Cortina. Glass thrust the paper through the window at their young driver. " Take us there quickly. Hang on, where's Slade?"

" Over at the Post Office taking photographs," pointed Moon.

" Get him, will you. I promised he could come. And hurry up. I'm not looking forward to this and I don't want pneumonia as well."

SIX

The night passed.

There was no news of the Post Office robbers.

At Scotland Yard, Detective Chief Inspector Glass, with the aid of Sergeant Moon, sifted through files and reports until 1 a.m. They found nothing of immediate value and eventually returned to their respective homes.

Mr. and Mrs. Lucas, having failed to pick out the thieves' pictures in the Rogues Gallery, slept fitfully back at their Leyton Post Office.

Carol Spencer slept better, in a drugged sleep at a Middlesex hospital where she had been given sedatives after the shock of seeing her husband's body in the mortuary. Her daughter, Fiona, stayed at home with her grandparents. Her late husband, Michael, stiffened in his plastic coffin.

The early morning editions leaving the Fleet Stret offices of *The Megaphone* carried Timothy Slade's front page appeal to find the getaway car.

Police throughout the country kept a lookout for old Fords.

In Wormwood Scrubs, Robert Trevellyn spent the first long night of his seven-year sentence for the murder of a defenceless old man.

And at 2 a.m., in the heart of London, The Executioner claimed his first victim.

SEVEN

Alfred George Debbings, known nefariously as Debbings The Pipes, was released from Wormwood Scrubs at 11 a.m. on Thursday March 11th. He owed his quaint soubriquet to his custom of climbing drainpipes in order to gain illegal entry into property. His last attempt three years ago had not been successful. As he was stealthily returning to the open bedroom window with the old family silver, the old Lord had woken up and made the mistake of challenging him.

Debbings had not meant to hit His Lordship quite so hard with the candelabra, and possibly some portion of blame could be attributed to the egg-shell fragility of the noble skull. However, the sound of the blow had wakened the entire household who collectively managed to prevent Debbing's departure, and only the expertise of a clever lawyer had been able to get the charge reduced to manslaughter.

Now, three years later, Debbings was a free man again.

His first day out of prison was uneventful. On release he took a taxi to Paddington where he rented a room in one of the seedy terraced lodging-houses that surround the station. Here he lived in sin with a common Clapham whore called Hazel, a heavily-built woman who had since relinquished her commercial career for a daytime job behind a till at Safeways, although she still did the occasional foreigner. Often an Arab.

It was not a luxurious room. The striped horsehair mattress on the iron bed boasted an unpleasant brown stain; rusting springs bulged the moquette of a green three-piece suite, and the cold water tap dripped montonously into the cracked washbasin like a liquid metronome.

Debbings did not care. His life had been spent in a succession of similar furnished rooms interspersed by periods in Her Majesty's institutions which were marginally more comfortable. He supplemented his generous income from the Social Security with the proceeds from his career as a Master Burgler.

He was the right shape for Master Burglary. He stood only five feet five inches tall, and his eight and a half stone frame could be easily squeezed serpent fashion through tiny bathroom and pantry windows. But three years in prison had taken the edge off his fitness. Although still only forty-one, his pasty cheeks, red veins and dandruff marked him out as a man little acquainted with fresh air, sobriety or health foods.

He worked alone. Most of his information he gleaned from gossip in middle-class pubs, and from milkmen and delivery men who were able to tell him when the occupants of certain houses would be away and which of them were worth breaking into. On the occasion of his last job, his information had let him down.

Discarding his prison clothes, Debbings selected his best suit from the peeling walnut wardrobe. This was a grey worsted bought from John Colliers when they were the Fifty Shilling Tailors, and it matched his complexion well. With it he wore a purple shirt, heliotrope tie and black shoes (which he wiped over with the sleeve of his best suit), a colour combination happily covered by a dirty white trenchcoat with torn epaulettes, of the type worn by Alan Ladd in " The Blue Dahlia " in 1947.

Thus attired, Debbings ventured out onto the streets of London. He took lunch in a snack bar in Praed Street where he studied the racing pages of *The Megaphone* over a salt-beef sandwich and a cup of milky tea from a plastic cup. He had not yet decided what he was going to do with his new-found freedom. There were no spoils waiting to be divided and no friends waiting to offer him new jobs. He had little money but did not contemplate regular employment. The Social Security had always looked after him adequately in the past, and he saw no reason to be disloyal to them now. Until then he would live off the earnings of his woman.

He turned to Page Five in the newspaper for the daily nude model. Juliette, a model who spoke five languages, liked ski-ing and had a degree in Further Economics, had elongated nipples that reminded Debbings of the mushrooms in the prison dinners.

Finishing his lunch, he wandered down the Edgware Road towards Marble Arch where he turned left into Oxford Street, fighting his way through the early Easter shoppers. Selfridges windows featured fashions, household goods and toys carefully displayed in giant cracked-open Easter Eggs.

Passing Oxford Circus, he reached Soho, just in time to put

twenty-five pence each way on Son et Lumière in the four o'clock race at Carlisle. The bookmakers was packed with Soho personalities, clip joint bouncers, market traders, a denim-clad street musician with his acoustic guitar hoisted on his back and a couple of black reggae singers from the nearby offices of a major record company.

The bookmaker called last bets for the race as the radio announced the horses under starters orders at Carlisle.

A few miles away at Leyton, two men were robbing a Post Office.

Debbings did not stay for the result of the race but continued on his aimless meanderings, through the maze of crowded cosmopolitan streets until he came to Soho Square. By now the cold March wind was joined by a swirling mist, and droplets of dew were forming on the grass around the black and white pagoda. The thin trenchcoat offered little protection, and Debbings shivered. It would be six-thirty at least before his woman came home, later if she had gone out after work. He decided to go to a cinema.

He chose the Classic in Charing Cross Road which was showing " Sexy Lovers " and " Swedish Girls Do ", a combination of programme which rekindled in him certain desires which had been necessarily repressed for the past thirty-six months. Having seen both films once, he treated himself to an ice cream and saw " Sexy Lovers " again. Most of his fellow voyeurs were men, and the cinema smelt of a mixture of drying clothes, cigarette smoke and stale semen. There was little conversation in the audience.

He came out of the cinema at ten-thirty. In a litter bin outside Leicester Square tube station he found an *Evening Standard* which he took into a nearby coffee bar. Here, an effeminate Spaniard served him with a greasy ham omelette and lukewarm coffee in a plastic beaker.

The stop press in the *Standard* carried an item about the Post Office Robbery and the killing of a policeman, but Debbings was more interested in the racing results. Son et Lumière had won at 7-2.

It was his last piece of good fortune.

Finishing his meal he made for Rupert Street. Soho was beginning to come alive. Burly bouncers in evening dress stood outside the strip clubs cajoling likely punters to part with their money; names appeared alongside doorbells, paper promises of promiscuous pleasure—(" Denise, French polishing; Cath, Strict Lessons; Eve, Rubber Garments to Measure "). Foreign restaurants, each sporting red lighting, trailing plastic flowers and Continental musak, vied for the respectable couples trade.

Debbings was neither respectable nor a couple. He stopped outside a doorway where a cracked illuminated sign promised an " Evening Extravaganza of Naked Nubile Beauty ". In exchange for two pounds he was conducted down an entry where, for a further three pounds " membership " he faced some steep steps into a dingy cellar. Here he joined a group of men sitting on upright wooden chairs in front of a small stage. Most of the men were Japanese. For the next hour and a half he watched a succession of girls with prominent rib cages and bored eyes speedily remove their clothes beneath the 200-watt bulb that passed as a spotlight.

When the last G-string was discarded, he wandered to the bar and bought a diluted double whisky for two pounds.

At 1 a.m. he left the club and slouched along the shadows of the Soho alleys. The night was cold and misty. Wooden crates, the debris of the day's markets, lined the sides of the pavements awaiting collection. He kicked a sodden cardboard box aside.

Which was when he became aware of the footsteps behind him because they quickened too.

Debbings turned round sharply. The man in the black overcoat, however, made no effort to hide.

" Mr. Debbings?"

Debbings peered cautiously at the stranger. The cultured voice and upright bearing suggested a person of position. He racked his brains to remember if this was some policeman he should recognise.

" We haven't met, Mr. Debbings, but I have a job for you. Can we talk somewhere?"

" Not me, mate. You must 'ave the wrong bloke."

" I don't think so, Mr. Debbings. It's worth a oner."

Debbings was suspicious. It could be a frame. " A oner? Are you joking? I wouldn't get out of bed for a oner." He was playing for time.

" I didn't know they had increased the pay out at the Scrubs. I reckon you could well use a hundred pounds right now, Mr. Debbings."

So the man knew that he had come out of prison that day.

" Come with me where we can discuss it." He indicated a blue saloon parked at the corner. Reluctantly, Debbings followed and was shown into the front passenger seat. They drove through Piccadilly Circus, down the Haymarket to Trafalgar Square and into St. James's Park.

Debbings noticed that the car had real leather seats. One of those foreign jobs probably. The man must have some cash with wheels like this. He tried to make out the driver's features, but the upturned coat collar got in his way every time they passed beneath a street lamp.

The car pulled up at the back of the Barracks in the park.

48

"Let's take a walk, shall we, Mr. Debbings, and I can outline my plan." He jumped out of the car, walked round to the passenger side and opened the door for the Master Burglar. "You could become a very important man, you know. Your name on every front page." He helped the nervous criminal from the vehicle and almost pushed him into the park, across the bridge over the lake and along a path leading deep into the shrubbery, hidden by trees and foliage.

"I think this is far enough," said the man pleasantly. "Now first of all, I want to talk to you about your last job. Not very successful I believe?"

Debbings looked uncomfortable. Three years in gaol hardly constituted a good reference for future prospective employers.

"It was my snout, wasn't it? Gave me the wrong info."

"Oh yes?" The man retained his tone of polite interest.

"Yeah. Told me the whole family had gone away, but half the staff were there and the old geezer himself caught me with the goods. I had to slug him, didn't I?"

"Oh, undoubtedly. Er, need you have slugged him quite so hard?"

"Not my fault the old boy croaked. I didn't know he couldn't take it."

"You don't feel sorry that you killed him then?" There was a new sharp edge to the voice, but Debbings did not notice it.

"Do me a favour. Would you feel sorry for someone who got you three years in stir?" He was not sure where this line of questioning was leading, but he thought he had better impress the man with his mettle. "So I hit him a bit hard. But I got off, didn't I? I had Old Fowler defending me and he had the jury in the palms of his hands."

" He fooled them, did he?" The man laughed, but his eyes were cold. Debbings could not see his eyes in the dark and laughed too.

" I should say so," he chortled.

The man stopped laughing suddenly. " Have you any relatives, Mr. Debbings?"

" Only an old aunt in Sussex. Here, what's all this getting at?"

" I just wondered, my friend, to whom you will be leaving your money."

" I ain't got no money." For the first time the little crook began to perceive something not quite right about the conversation. " Here, what do you mean, leaving my money?"

" I regret that you will not be with us much longer, Mr. Debbings."

" What do you mean? Who are you?" Debbings was suddenly afraid. He started to run, but a gloved hand reached out and effortlessly gripped his thin neck.

" It is who YOU are that matters, Debbings, and you are a brutal murderer. You killed a very good man, a man who had done no harm to you. I had to be sure that you felt no remorse. You think you have made a fool of the law, but I tell you that now *I* am the law and this time justice shall be done."

" I didn't mean to kill him."

" But you don't care that you did."

A second hand fastened round the burglar's throat, choking off the cry that was rising there. Debbing's hands tried to free himself from the grip, but the pressure on his windpipe was weakening him and a pain in his head was blacking everything out. He felt like he was falling off a cliff and with a violent thud hit the bottom.

The man moved quickly as Debbings sank unconscious

at his knees. From his deep pockets he took a length of nylon rope and tied a noose which he fitted neatly over the burglar's Adam's apple. " It will take a while for you to die," he said conversationally as he pulled the other end of the rope over the branch of a nearby tree. As soon as Debbing's feet cleared the floor he stopped pulling and secured the rope to the trunk. " Pierrepoint was much quicker than I. Would you care for the Last Rites?"

But Debbings was past hearing. His eyes had started to bulge out of his puffed red face. His lips were turning blue like his veins. Breath was still forced through his lips, but spittle ran down the side of his mouth. He could not swallow. A gust of wind caught his flapping grey worsted jacket and swung his useless body to and fro like a pendulum of offal.

The man took a small card from his pockets and pinned it carefully to the lapel of Debbing's open trenchcoat. Printed on the card was a black gallows.

Perhaps a trifle theatrical, thought the man, as he made his way back to his car. But it would be good publicity. And if there was one thing The Executioner wanted it was publicity.

It was 3 a.m. as he drove unnoticed through the gates of St. James's Park and disappeared in the direction of Marble Arch. Eleven hours since the Post Office Robbery had taken place.

And the same time as the missing Ford Executive was discovered by a police patrol car in Blackpool.

EIGHT

Friday, March 12th.

Detective Chief Inspector Glass woke at six with yellow fur on his tongue and a loud knocking noise in his head. He reached sleepily across to the bedside table for his cigarettes, nearly overturning the cracked glass tumbler that held his top teeth. He lit a Craven A, sucked the smoke deep into his lungs and coughed at some length until he was able to regurgitate a wad of thick green phlegm.

The knocking grew louder, and he realised that someone was at the door. Clutching his striped winceyette pyjamas around his waist, he switched on the light cord and stumbled into his tiny hall to open the front door. On the threshold stood a large, blowsy woman of late middle age. Her bosom, unharnessed beneath her flannel dressing-gown, overhung her stomach by inches, metal curlers were dotted atop her tight grey perm like landmines and her breath smelt strongly of stale gin. She glared at the detective through red eyes.

" Telephone for you, Mr. Glass." She clicked her tongue in disapproval. " At this time, too."

Holding on to his pyjamas cord, Glass hopped back across the room, inserted his dentures, put on his slippers and followed the woman down the stairs.

" Sorry about this, Mrs. Cowan. Not often they ring at this time. I'm afraid mine is out of order." He wished hers had been out of order as well then he might have got his eight hours' sleep.

"It's not good enough, disturbing a woman's rest." The slattern disappeared into the ground-floor flat leaving the detective alone in the lofty main hall beside the wall-mounted telephone.

"Hello. Detective Chief Inspector Glass here."

It was Scotland Yard. They informed him of the recovery of the Ford Executive and requested his early presence in Whitehall.

"I will be over immediately," coughed Glass.

He made his way back up the lino-covered stairs. By the adroit use of plasterboard, seven flats had been constructed within the ageing walls of this decaying Victorian villa, the Inspector's two rooms and kitchen taking up the space of the former attic.

The rooms were comfortably, rather than luxuriously, furnished. Oak was the dominant wood, recurring in the draw-leaf table, the bulky sideboard and the bedroom suite. A red hearthrug covering the Wilton carpet matched the red moquette three-piece suite, and the lounge was warmed by a teak-framed gas fire. There was no trace of a woman anywhere in the flat.

Glass dressed quickly, choosing a brown herringbone suit, made himself a cup of strong tea and a round of toast with Wensleydale cheese and packed his briefcase for the journey.

He ate the last pieces of toast as he hurried, head down, to the corrugated iron garage built at the side of the house to protect the inhabitants from stray German bombs. Inside, wet from the night's rain dripping through the roof, stood his car, a grey 1957 Austin A35, obsolete forerunner of the Mini.

He started it with a rusty handle at the third attempt

53

and, amidst a cloud of smoke that indicated burning oil and worn pistons, he drove off to the New Scotland Yard building at Westminster.

The Assistant Commissioner was waiting for him in his office.

"Sorry to drag you in so early, Walter," he apologised insincerely. "Especially after your late night, but we have to pull out all the stops on this one. The getaway car has been found on the Golden Mile at Blackpool."

"Where?"

"Behind a bingo stall. We've had it checked out. It was stolen from the Walthamstow area yesterday lunchtime. It has got to be the same one."

"I wonder why Blackpool?" mused Glass. "The illuminations aren't on."

"That's up to you to find out, and Walter," the A.C. put his arm on Glass's shoulder, "tie it up quickly, eh? Public opinion and all that."

"You forget, I was the one who broke the news to P.C. Spencer's wife." Glass disengaged himself from his superior's unwelcome embrace. "Who is looking after the car now?"

"The Lancashire police. Their forensic boys are working on it at this moment."

Glass glanced out of the window. It was still dark. He picked up the Assistant Commissioner's telephone without permisison and spoke to the duty room switchboard officer. "Detective Chief Inspector Glass here. Send a car round to Sergeant Moon's house immediately and have him brought to my office. And tell the car to wait for us." He replaced the receiver and checked the time on the gold hunter he always wore with his herringbone suit. Ten to seven.

"Your train leaves Euston at 7.45 a.m. A car will pick you up in Preston."

" Right. I've one or two things to do in my office." Glass descended by lift to his own floor. A pile of papers swayed on his ' in ' tray as he opened his door. He picked them up, groaned, and put them down again. He went back to the corridor and stopped by a vending machine, inserted 5p and pressed the button for sugarless, milkless tea. The liquid trickled down, but unhappily was not preceded by a paper cup and merely ran into the waste. Glass kicked the machine, lit a Craven A and returned to his office. Minutes later, Moon arrived looking tired, dishevelled and bewildered.

" Let's go, son," said Glass. " We are off to the seaside." He hurried the sergeant down to the waiting vehicle and delivered curt instructions to the driver. " Euston Station. You've got thirty minutes, so step on it."

" Hold tight then," nodded the driver. " Do you want the siren on?"

" If it will get us there any quicker, you can play the Trumpet Voluntary," said Glass.

They reached the Station with ten minutes to spare. The Euston concourse was packed. Early morning business men with earnest faces and furled umbrellas walked stiffly from platform to taxi, vying for space with young couples with large cases, clinging to one another in tearful valediction. Children cried, trolleys rattled and, above all the noise, the loudspeaker boomed " The train in Platform 12 is the 7.45 for Glasgow calling at Rugby, Preston and Carlisle. Passengers for Blackpool change at Preston."

" That's us," said Glass. " I'll just go and get a paper."

He pushed his way through the crowd to the John Menzies bookstall, Moon behind him, and bought *The Megaphone* and the *Reveille*. Moon bought the *Daily Telegraph* and a packet of Rennies. " I travel badly," he explained. The barriers were closing as they showed their warrant cards and trotted briskly to the nearest second-class carriage halfway down the train.

" In the old days we would have had a first-class compartment to ourselves," grumbled Glass as he settled down beside a young Scottish woman with two small children and a Tartan hold-all. The sergeant sat opposite.

Glass opened his paper and studied the headlines. Timothy Slade had done him proud. The economic crises, the Middle East crisis and the British Leyland crisis had all been relegated to the inner pages and a photograph of the tearful Carol Spencer being helped to the ambulance (taken discreetly by Timothy from the police car window) was blown up alongside the front page report.

Even the Editor had done his bit. The leader column emphasised the urgent need for an immediate improvement in police pay in view of the dangerous nature of the job. Timothy Slade's own article was detailed and accurate, and it finished off by reassuring the public that a senior Scotland Yard officer, Detective Chief Inspector Walter Glass, was in charge of the case and optimistic of an early arrest.

Glass winced on reading this, put down the paper and slept for the rest of the journey. The train pulled into Preston shortly before eleven o'clock. The two detectives walked slowly up the slope from Platform 6 to the main exit. An orange and white Jaguar with POLICE emblazoned on every panel was waiting alongside the taxis. As they walked over a uniformed officer jumped out.

" Detective Chief Inspector Glass is it ?"

Glass nodded. " And this is Sergeant Moon."

" Constable Makepeace, sir. I have the car here to take you to H.Q."

" So I notice," said Glass, climbing into the back seat.

A watery sun filtered through the window as they drove along the A583 dual carriageway towards the resort. The journey took only twenty minutes, but well before they reached Blackpool they could see the steel girders of the famous Tower rising in the distance beyond the fields like a giant Meccano penis. As they drove along the Promenade, a fierce wind blew spray from the sea over the railings and onto the tramlines.

" Bracing, isn't it?" said Moon.

" This is nothing. The sea comes right over the Promenade some days."

Out of season, the Golden Mile was like a forsaken shanty town, but much activity was going on behind the scenes in preparation for Easter.

" Not like it used to be," vouchsafed Constable Makepeace, who suddenly assumed the mantle of courier. " One time it was all open-air stalls. Wooden huts with fortune tellers, Kentucky Derby and whelks and cockles. Now it is giant indoor electronic complexes. The human touch has gone."

Glass, who could have written a four-volume book echoing similar sentiments lamented that indeed it had.

" At least we have kept the trams which is more than anywhere else in England has." He turned off the road before they reached the Tower. " Here we are, sir. The Ford is in that car park behind the bingo palace. Inspector Moorcroft from our C.I.D. is there. He is in charge of things at this end."

They pulled up beside the rusting Ford Executive which was surrounded by forensic experts like a gaggle of Jewish tailors looking for a flaw in a suit.

A man with luxuriant side-whiskers was waiting to open their door. " I am Detective Inspector Moorcroft," he

57

boomed. "You must be Glass." He grasped the detective's arm and hauled him out of the car. They shook hands and introduced their respective sergeants, Sherlock and Moon. Sherlock and Moon warily exchanged nods. They all turned up their coat collars to shield themselves from the gale.

"We are pretty sure it is the same car they used," said Moorcroft, getting straight down to business. "Belongs to a Mr. David Cope of Walthamstow. Stolen yesterday lunchtime. I've checked him out. He's O.K. A librarian at Epping." Moorcroft had a staccato way of speaking, not unlike a teleprinter. Glass half expected to see the tape coming out of his ears.

"You soon found it," he said.

"Smart lads up here you know. Patrol drives round the car parks every night. Doors were wide open. Obviously suspicious. They checked with the computer, and thirty seconds later they realised. The car the whole country was looking for."

"And what have you found in it so far?"

"Ah, well, nothing I'm afraid. Professionals I would say. No prints, nothing like that. No trace of anything at all really."

"All we could expect."

Inspector Moorcroft coughed discreetly. "Might I ask exactly what you will be doing up here? You are very welcome, don't get me wrong. I know it is your case. What line of enquiry are you following?"

Glass looked sharply at Moon who turned away to admire the Victorian architectural splendour of the Tower.

"I shall wander about, ask a few questions. Nobody knows me round here. They will be off their guard. I might hear something that your lads wouldn't."

Moorcroft looked doubtful. "Possibly. You are working

on the assumption then that these are local villains?"

"Well, they must have had some reason for coming to Blackpool."

"Yes, of course. Well, maybe you would care for some lunch now? I thought we might go to the Imperial. We have booked you in there for this evening, so we can kill two birds with one stone."

The Imperial Hotel stood in palatial grandeur overlooking the North Promenade. The police party pushed their way through the revolving doors into the vast opulent lounge. The walls were dark panelled, glass chandeliers hung from the ceiling, and illuminated showcases displayed expensive goods from local traders.

Glass led the way to the reception desk. "We'll leave our bags upstairs and join you in the restaurant."

"What are you really going to do in Blackpool?" asked Moon when they reached the sanctuary of their twin-bedded room.

Glass walked over to the window and stared at the white waves of the Irish Sea crashing against the walls of the Promenade below. "Like I say. Look around, ask a few questions." He unpacked his executive briefcase and hung his spare suit in the wardrobe.

"I see," said Moon, who did not see at all. "Just look around and . . ."

"Ask a few questions."

"Mmmmm."

The afternoon was spent at Police Headquarters where a meeting of officers had been set up to discuss the case in depth. It was officially described as a "think tank", and it bored Glass immensely. He tried to concentrate, but his mind kept meandering. He wondered how Sherlock Holmes would have tackled the case. Probably he would have found rare cigar ash on the car seat and deduced the robbers were Indonesian gas board inspectors living in high rise flats in East Kilbride. Glass did not think Holmes would have fared well in the police. Individuality was discouraged as being too like eccentricity. Then again, the flapping of his hat round his ears would have caused some distraction. He jerked his mind to the present.

The Blackpool contingent were discussing which of their regular jailbirds could be likely contenders for the Post Office robberies.

" There is Little Johnny Owen," suggested a nameless C.I.D. sergeant.

" Still in Walton," said Moorcroft, the warm room making his jowls a brighter red against the white side-whiskers like a Dickensian Father Christmas. " For the Shuttle job. A hold-up at a Lytham bank," he explained proudly to Glass, as if to emphasise that London had not got a monopoly on big-time crime.

Glass smiled agreeably in an Alistair Sim sort of way and wished they would let him go to sleep. He did not even have a cigarette.

The names of Alec Clacker, Roger Bruford and Jumping John Roscoe were mentioned and dropped. No decisions were made and the meeting broke up inconclusively around tea time. Glass knew it would. The killer of Michael Spencer would not be found by sitting around in overheated police stations. He wanted to be talking *to* the local hoodlums, not about them. He could not wait for the evening so that he could get into the town and fraternise with them. That was where the leads would come from, not from " think tanks ". He laughed scornfully as he searched in his pocket for a cigarette then remembered he was out of them.

" Is there anywhere round here I can buy some Craven

A?" he asked.

"Craven A?" said Moorcroft. "I haven't seen a packet of those for years."

"Really?" said Glass maliciously. "Everyone in London smokes them."

"I think I'll stick to Menthol." He proferred a packet of Consulate. "Care for one?"

Glass screwed up his face and watched as Moorcroft flicked uselessly at a tarnished petrol lighter. "Allow me," he said, striking a Swan Vesta.

"Keep meaning to have the thing mended. Little chap in Victoria Street does them. Very good he is."

"Matches don't need mending," murmured Glass enigmatically.

Moorcroft exhaled acrid fumes. "What are your plans for tonight then?"

"I believe there is a club beneath this hotel?"

"That's right, Trader Jacks. More a high-class discotheque really."

Trader Jacks opened at ten, and Glass and Moon were in for ten-thirty. The club boasted a swimming pool, jungle foliage and a black disc jockey who played all the currently fashionable funky disco sounds. Moon was pleased to see a group of businessmen at the bar, refugees from a hotel conference. He felt they made Glass look less conspicuous amongst the young jet-setters. His superior officer hardly had the suave image of a Cary Grant or David Niven that would have enabled him to carry his age. In his baggy check suit, dotted tie and brown toe-caps, Glass was cast more in the Walter Brennan mould. Moon thought he could be mistaken for his grandfather.

They sipped drinks quietly at the bar until the dance floor filled, then Glass turned to Moon. "Right. Are you ready?"

Moon drained his half of lager. "Are we off?"

"No. We're dancing. Come on." Glass led the way and stopped beside two girls with long blonde hair, tight jeans and artificial smiles. He tapped the nearest one on the shoulder and, as she turned round, broke into a jerking motion that, in the dim light, could have been construed as dancing. Moon, more bashful, asked permission of the other to join her. She continued dancing wordlessly without a flicker of greeting in her fixed grin so that Moon just wriggled his hips alongside, thinking that if she turned away he could always pretend he was dancing with someone else. No one would notice on the packed floor.

They lasted for the duration of Candi Staton's "Young Hearts Run Free" whereupon the girls said "Thank you" in practised unison and swept sweetly away to another part of the club.

"There are two more over there," said Glass relentlessly. "I'll have the good-looking one with the thick lips. Yours is the short fat one." He moved in on them with seasoned strides. It was a far cry from Mrs. Lethwaite. They danced for three records. Moon managed to elicit from his the information that she was a shorthand typist at the Provincial Building Society and liked being taken out for expensive meals. He was not impressed with this and was relieved when Glass marched off the dance floor.

"If you don't mind me saying so, sir, I don't see how we are gaining anything from this," he panted as he rejoined the Inspector by the bar.

"Fun, though, isn't it?" leered Glass.

Moon could think of no suitable riposte. The Inspector's tone changed. "I also found out, Sergeant, from the last young lady, who incidentally without her make-up would

62

be nearer my age than yours, the addresses of a dozen clubs in this town where I am more likely to find what I am looking for." He sucked the last drop of Southern Comfort from his glass. "And it is to these that I am going now."

"Am I coming?"

"No, I work better alone. You get some sleep. You look as though you need it. See you tomorrow." And he was gone.

Moon went straight to his room, certainly tired after his train journey, his long afternoon conference and his five hours' sleep the night before. He did not know how Glass kept it up, especially at his age.

He switched on the bedside TV in his room. Just in time for the Late Night News on BBC2. For the first time he learnt of the murder of Alfred Debbings, the first victim of The Executioner. Moon listened to the rest of the report, but little information was given. Detective Chief Inspector Knox was said to be leading exhaustive enquiries.

Moon turned the set off at his bedside console and slid under the covers. Outside, the gales still howled. Sleepily he wondered how Knox was progressing.

NINE

The reproduction antique telephone standing on the onyx bedside table rang loudly. Outside the casement windows, birds sang in the upper branches of the Portman Square plane trees. An arm encased in red silk pyjamas emerged from beneath the brown continental quilt, took off the receiver and pulled it under the bedclothes.

" Knox."

It was Scotland Yard, imparting the information that one Alfred George Debbings had been discovered hanging from a tree in St. James's Park. The body had been discovered by a tramp called August Johnny and identified by a diary in the suit pocket. It was now 9.45 a.m. Would Detective Chief Inspector Knox kindly be at the Yard by ten.

" No," Knox told them, " he would not. They could send a car with his sergeant to pick him up. He would expect it in fifteen minutes. He replaced the receiver firmly.

Robin Knox was thirty-five. He had risen quickly in the Force since his graduation from police college, a rise that had not gone unnoticed by men of the old school like Detective Chief Inspector Glass who believed that three weeks treading a beat in Limehouse was worth three years sat behind a " school desk ".

Knox had a quick shower and prepared himself a bowl of All Bran, Bemax, Force wheat flakes and honey mixed with hot milk and a raw egg. His usual breakfast. He ate it in the lounge, a room tastefully furnished in Art Deco style with a giant Biba settee, smoked glass dining-set and a number of goatskin rugs covering the polished pine floor. A Beng & Oulson stereo took pride of place on the wall unit beneath a bookshelf filled with philosophical volumes by Colin Wilson.

The police car arrived at 10.07. He put the dishes into the dishwasher when the Entryphone buzzed and went straight down in the lift.

" Morning, sir." His sergeant, a broad man in his early forties, greeted him.

" Morning, Evans. Get you out of bed, did they?"

"Oh no. I have been up since seven. When you have small children, sir."

Knox grimaced. "So they tell me."

"Have a good night yourself, did you, sir?" The Chief Inspector's social habits were much discussed at the Yard. He was as likely to appear in the columns of Nigel Dempster as in the *Police Gazette*.

"Not bad. Ended up at Tramps. Met a rather nice girl actually. I am seeing her tonight, work permitting."

Detective Sergeant Evans stood back to let Knox into the car first. "Well, it looks like a big one this time, sir. The one we have all been waiting for—The Executioner."

"Really?" Knox was eager now. He had believed the letter was a hoax, but if it proved to be genuine then this was a very good case for him to get. Public interest had been high since the letter was first published so he would be in the limelight from the start.

At the Yard they called him 'Opportunity' Knox.

When they reached St. James's Park, Debbing's body had been cut down from the tree and laid on the path beside the shrubbery surrounded by the whole production team that had been evident at Leyton the day before.

The Police Surgeon sought him out. "He died from strangulation. He was probably unconscious when he was strung up, but he did not actually die until quite a bit later. We shall know the exact time from the post mortem."

"I shall be going along to the mortuary myself."

"This was pinned to the lapel." He handed across the card with the imprint of the gallows. "This is why we believe it is The Executioner."

"Anything found on the clothing?"

"Yes, sir." A young constable with dandruff came up. It was his first murder case and he was full of self-importance. "A Yale key and a diary in his suit. That's where we got his name, sir."

"Yes, yes, go on."

"In his raincoat, sir, we found half a cinema ticket, an *Evening Standard* of last night's, a soiled handkerchief, a betting-slip from a bookie in Soho and about six pounds in cash."

"Good. I'll take the diary and the key. Do we know the cinema?"

"A Classic I believe, sir."

"Right," said Knox. "Let's get the show rolling then. I shall want statements from the lab. boys, the fingerprint men and this tramp that found the body. Have we been in touch with the traffic patrols who were round this area last night? We shall want to know all Debbing's movements and contacts since he left the Scrubs, where he is living and who with. And where is this Pathologist?" He strode down the path importantly, his thick blond hair haloed by the sun giving him an Adonis-like appearance. He had an "I'll get something done" air about him which impressed the acolytes in his entourage.

It would not have impressed Detective Chief Inspector Glass. He would have preferred to sit and wait for Eddie The Nose.

Sue Owen approached Paddington Tube Station via the Praed Street entrance. She stopped to buy a *Daily Mail* from the street newsvendor, collected a yellow ticket from the automatic machine and descended the steps at the far end of the bridge that led to Platform Two, the eastbound Circle line. All around her, commuters were scurrying like iron filings under a moving magnet.

The rails rattled as the silver train emerged from the

tunnel into the brief section of open air. She surged towards the opening doors with the rest of the crowd and managed to grab the last remaining seat, opposite an elderly Chinese lady and a grey-faced stockbroker who spent the entire journey watching her bra-less breasts bounce in rhythm to the bogies.

She was a striking girl, very much of the seventies, with a Charlie's Angels haircut, skin-tight jeans and a T-shirt bearing a cartoon of a German warplane with the inscription DIRTY FOKKER printed above her provocatively protruding nipples. As a concession to the chilly March morning, a fur-lined denim jacket covered her shoulders.

She travelled three stations to Kensington High Street (ex. Biba; ex. Derry & Toms; home of hippies, bohemians and eccentrics; Bedsitland; tourist paradise; world of antique dealers) and rose on the steep escalator to ground level.

She worked on a stall in the Antique Hypermarket in the High Street. Her boss, a wealthy Greek, whose main shop was in Hastings, visited the premises only a couple of times a week thus leaving Sue to run the business almost single-handed.

The stall opened at 10 a.m., so Sue was in good time, which was a miracle in itself considering that the night before she had been dancing at Tramps Discotheque in Jermyn Street until 3 a.m.

"Have a good night, Sue?" asked the French girl on the next stall as Sue opened the shutters. The French girl sold "antiques" of the fifties, Dinky cars, School Friend Annuals, Coronation mugs, etc. Her name was Hélène.

"Not bad. Met this bloke, an inspector at Scotland Yard."

"Oh yes? And what happened to the Fleet Street Fop

67

then?"

"He's tomorrow. This one is quite nice. He's got," she sought the word, "charisma. You know, I'm sure I've seen him mentioned in the papers."

"What's his name?"

"Robin Knox. He's taking me for tea at Selfridges."

"The hotel or the snack bar?"

"The hotel I hope." She picked up the morning mail. "Yes, he's quite dishy, but I don't know how I shall fit him in. Tim wants me to go up to the Lakes with him this weekend."

"You'll manage," said Hélène. "You always have before."

The day passed quickly. She lunched at the snack bar inside the Hypermarket, a converted railway carriage complete with the original G.W.R. seats and fittings including the framed photographs of sepia seaside resorts and water colours of old railway locomotives.

At 5 p.m. she caught a 73 bus which took thirty-five minutes to reach Bond St., crawling through the rush-hour traffic in Knightsbridge, Park Lane and Oxford Street.

She arrived breathlessly at the main entrance to Selfridges Hotel and walked through the automatic opening doors. No sign of Robin Knox. She rushed to the Ladies on the First Floor to make running repairs to her face and hair, and cursed Farrah Fawcett-Majors when she looked in the mirror. The style might look good on TV, but it was not holding up well to the blustery rigours of an English winter. She combed it the best she could, renewed her lip gloss, pinched her nipples for effect, and made her entrance to the lounge. Robin Knox was waiting beside a reproduction writing-table. He allowed her to walk towards him.

"I saw you running upstairs," he greeted her. Her knees

went weak like a Jilly Cooper heroine.

"You are late," she accused, recovering her savoir-faire. "I might have had another date at six."

"I am seven minutes late and I can't even stay very long, so you will have plenty of time for it. I have left my sergeant driving round the block."

"What's happened? A bank robbery?"

"A murder."

"Ooooh, where?" But Knox was not given to discussing his work.

"You can read about it in the evening paper. Will you come to my flat at eleven?"

She of a thousand lovers looked shocked. Men were usually a little more circuitous. "Just like that?"

"Just like that." He handed her a card. "Here is the address. I have a date at six too. With a Paddington prostitute. See you later?" He smiled. He had teeth like John Kennedy. He leaned down and kissed her suddenly on the lips. Then he was gone. A tang of Aramis hung in the air in his wake. Sue looked at her watch. Only five hours to go to eleven.

Sergeant Evans had completed only one circuit of the block when his superior returned.

"Get what you wanted?" he asked as he edged the car forward towards Oxford Street.

"I shall do later," smiled Knox. "Paddington next stop, Evans."

It had been a successful day. Fingerprints had soon confirmed that the body had been Alfred George Debbings. At the Soho bookmakers, the clerk inspected the betting-slip and offered Knox one pound, thirty-five pence.

"Your mate's already paid the tax," he explained.

" What time was he in ?"

The clerk checked the number in his ledger. " I'd say he backed this right on the off. Must have had a premonition."

They soon found that the Classic Cinema was the one in Charing Cross Road, and the manager there was able to tell them that the ticket had been issued at 4.30 p.m.

The post mortem had substantiated the Police Surgeon's opinion that Debbings had died from strangulation after hanging for some time at the end of the rope.

The diary had contained little information except an address in Paddington. Checking with the voters' list, Knox found it was the home of an Eric Snokes, Ivy Butterfield, Ian Butterfield, Hazel Hitchcock and Fred Fowler. There was no mention of an Alfred Debbings.

" He could have been living with somebody," said Knox, and an officer who had been at Debbing's trial confirmed that a woman was with him at the time.

" Word had it that he was living on her immoral earnings," said this officer. " He might have gone back to her, but we've no record who it was."

The prison had. One Hazel Hitchcock had visited Debbings in prison at spasmodic intervals during his three years' internment.

" Let's hope she is in," said Knox as they turned round Marble Arch and headed up Edgware Road.

" Bit early for the evening trade yet," said Evans.

They reached the house and were not impressed. " Hardly the international call-girl trade," commented the Inspector as he pushed the half-open door and knocked at the ground-floor flat.

An old man opened the door and eyed the detectives suspiciously. " What do you want ?" he wheezed. He wore a yellowing button-up vest over loose grey trousers.

" Police. We're looking for Hazel Hitchcock."

" Rozzers, eh? She's in the room up top?" He jerked a plastered thumb. " Can't you tell by the grooves on the stairs?"

" Has a lot of men in, does she?"

" Are you kidding. It's like the Eighth Army on the march some nights."

" Nice to see some of the self-employed are making a living under a Labour Government," said Knox. They walked up two flights of stairs and knocked at the only door. There was no reply.

" Give me that Yale key, Evans. This could be the lock it fits." He tried it, and it was. " We are in luck, Sergeant."

" We usually are, sir." They wandered round the shabby room.

" Here's something, sir." Evans held up a crumpled suit. " Prison issue. It looks as if he did come here first." He opened the wardrobe and sorted through the garments. " More of his stuff. No sign of a woman."

" She probably just uses it to bring her clients to."

Evans looked doubtfully at the bed. " I wouldn't fancy doing it on that thing. Look at that spring sticking out of the mattress. Some poor sod could get that right up the ass."

" And probably pay extra for it," said Knox.

" Do we wait then?"

" We'll have a word with the people at the bottom. They might know when she is likely to be in."

The man in the vest was reluctant to admit them, but Knox was insistent. His wife was more accommodating. " She works in Safeways at the daytime," she said in reply to Knox's question. " But she doesn't sleep here any more. Just entertains a few friends at night like."

71

" What we want to know, Mrs. Butterfield," said Knox who had read the nameplate outside the door, " is, have you seen a man go up there today?"

" No. But then, I'm out all day myself. What with all the shopping to do and Dad's prescription to get I'm hardly in before teatime."

" Has Mrs. Hitchcock lived here long?"

" About five years. She had a bloke, but he pissed off after the first year." The two officers exchanged glances. That would have been Debbings. Knox was about to ask her what time she got home when Mrs. Butterfield put her fingers to her lips. " Sssh. That could be her now."

Knox was first to the door, in time to see the spread of ample figure climbing the stairs.

" Mrs. Hitchcock?" he called out.

A husky Cockney voice floated down. " Hang on a minute, dearie. I'll do you in two shakes. I've got this gentleman to see to first."

Sergeant Evans smiled. " You'll have to wait your turn in the queue, sir."

" Unless you want to come up as well, luv. George here likes a double."

" She could probably accommodate another three if pressed," commented Knox starchly. " I wonder if she gives discount for bulk?" He called up the stairs. " I think I'll wait if it's all the same with George."

" Suit yourself, dear. I'll be down in ten minutes. He's only got a pound."

She was ready in five. " It must be inflation," said Evans as they walked upstairs in answer to her call, passing the small, bald George on the stairs like an outgoing batsman.

Mrs. Hitchcock was lying on her stomach on the bed when they walked in. Her bottom rose in the air like a

72

medium-sized hill. "Get yer clothes off, luv, and rinse it in the sink."

"I haven't come for that," said Knox in a tone of authority.

Hazel Hitchcock jumped to her feet. She wore a purple whalebone corset which restrained her ample form with difficulty. "What the hell . . ." she began, but Knox held up his hand.

"Don't get alarmed. We are only the police and we are not here to arrest you. All we want is a bit of information about one of your boy friends."

"Which one?" She made no attempt to cover herself. Evans observed her matching purple suspenders and wished his wife would get some. He did not find winceyette very enticing in bed.

"Alfred Debbings."

"Alfie. I haven't seen him in ages. He's inside."

"He came out yesterday."

"Did he? I knew it was about now, of course. Have you got a cigarette, luv?"

Knox did not smoke and ignored the question. "He was killed last night. Murdered. Don't you read the papers?"

"He wasn't? Not Alfie? Oh God! She started to sob, and her huge breasts wobbled like vanilla blancmanges as her body shook. Evans managed to touch the right one with his wrist as he leaned forward to offer her a handkerchief. It felt clammy. "When? How?" she spluttered.

Knox outlined the murder. Hazel Hitchcock listened, an incongruous figure now that reality had swept away the fantasy of her attire.

"We want to know who might have a reason for killing him."

She thought. "Nobody at all. He always worked on his

73

tod. Made little enough out of it, too. He weren't clever enough. But he never hurt no one. He was a pathetic little sod, really, was Alfie."

"It is not true to say he hurt nobody, Mrs. Hitchcock. In fact, he killed a man."

"That last time you mean? But that was an accident, I mean, Alfie just got panicky, didn't he? He only got done for manslaughter anyway."

"He was lucky."

"You think they might have something to do with it? The family of the bloke he killed? They might have a grudge."

"Lady Highly is seventy-six now. They had no children."

"Then someone he upset in prison?"

"You can't think of anyone yourself then?"

"I never see nobody who knows Alfie."

"When did you last see him?"

"A few months ago. I told him when he came out he could come back here and use the room. His things were here, just a few clothes that's all he had. But it was all over between us."

"He has been here, to change his clothes. Didn't you know?"

"I tell you, I ain't heard nothing from him for months. I only use this place at nights, it's handy for clients. I've got my own place at Clapham. Not much trade these days. Too many enthusiastic amateurs at it." She sounded surprised that anyone would ever want to go through the ordeal without payment. "Doing it for pleasure. Sure you don't want a quick one, luv?"

"I am afraid I know too many enthusiastic amateurs as you put it," said Knox. "And Sergeant Evans here has a wife and family to whom he is devoted, haven't you,

74

Sergeant Evans?" The Sergeant nodded. "Besides, he doesn't fancy your bed."

"We could always do it standing up," offered Hazel, but Evans declined gracefully.

"If you think of anything let us know," said Knox as they left. "Just ask for Detective Chief Inspector Knox at Scotland Yard."

"Where to now?" asked Evans as they got in the car.

"Home, I think. Tomorrow we shall go to Wormwood Scrubs and ask a few questions, but in the meantime I have a date with a beautiful young lady, and you, Sergeant Evans, have your wife and family to go home to."

In Blackpool, Detective Chief Inspector Glass was not so lucky.

TEN

The Establishment Club catered for the people who had been refused entry at every other club in Blackpool—the drunks, the queers, the trouble-makers, all of whom paid exorbitant prices for the privilege of being allowed in somewhere at last.

Sometimes, taxi drivers on commission would bring along innocent tourists, and their admission fees were determined by the hoodlum in evening dress on the door and varied according to their state of intoxication, reaching as much as ten pounds for alcoholics or foreigners unused to the currency. Glass, a sinister figure in his ex-army great-coat, paid twenty pence.

The interior of the club was bathed in an appropriate red glow, save for a corner stage where a grizzled guitarist sang Tex Ritter numbers beneath a single white spotlight. Lonely strangers hovered around the bar, eyes searching through the smoky gloom, but seeing only other lonely strangers looking back at them. It was as if all the marriage bureaux had ganged up and sent along their most difficult clients in the wild hope of getting them all off their hands in a sort of Cupid's Grand Slam.

Glass made a bee-line for the bar and stood posing as a lonely stranger. The counter was decorated in plywood strips, and a mural of the Swiss mountains on the wall behind suggested that the owners were trying to achieve a Tyrolean effect. He bought a Southern Comfort and reflected on how lucky Scotland Yard were to have a man with his drinking capacity on the squad for jobs such as these. Lesser officers would have been on their backs at this stage and it was still only half-past one.

So far he had visited seven clubs, and their names were fast becoming a blur. He could recall a voluminous blonde at Raffles and a funny comedian at the Tangerine. The Adam and Eve had made his head ache with the loud music and flashing lights, although he suspected it was his age. At Papa Jenks everyone had hair to their waist, and he had not been able to tell the girls from the boys. Or was that Mama Jenks? He really could not remember.

But it had not been a waste of time. In between his intakes of strong liquor he had talked to a lot of people, bought most of them drinks, listened to many more and made a number of acquaintances in the world of the Blackpool lawless.

For some reason, the men to whom he spoke were under the impression that Glass was a habitual criminal with a

76

particular talent for picking locks. He was agreeably surprised at the way they not only accepted his small deception but fell over themselves to offer him jobs. Indeed, were he ever to leave the police service he would have been able to make a comfortable living in Blackpool working for his new friends.

He had listened carefully whilst they mentioned various names in general conversation, and he eventually steered the talk to post office robberies and the Leyton job.

" I see they found the Ford in Blackpool. One of the local lads was it? You boys certainly get around. I tell you, they did well to get out of The Smoke those boys."

And he waited to see if the bait was taken, and one name cropped up on three occasions. Just casually, but it was the only name mentioned more than once.

" Sounds like a Patsy Kelly job. He used to live in Blackpool. Not seen him up here for a long time though."
" Do you ever remember Patrick Kelly, Patsy they used to call him. He was the man to take with you on a bank job." Only Bomber Chapman and Patsy Kelly were up to jobs like that."

Patsy Kelly. Left town over twelve months ago. Whereabouts unknown.

So Glass asked a few questions more. Casually. Intimating he had a job lined up and he needed some men. Someone had mentioned a Patsy Kelly.

And he came up with a girl's name—Eileen McNamara, ex-mistress of Mr. Kelly. Word had it they might still be in touch. She was said to hang around the Establishment Club. Did he know it?

Thus it was that Glass sipped his ninth Southern Comfort and looked across the red smog at the social rejects in the Establishment. He grinned happily to himself. This

77

was just his scene.

He had a fair description of the girl he was looking for. She was thirtyish with jet black hair done in an old-fashioned Dusty Springfield bouffant style, and she had an Irish lilt to her voice. One person referred to her as a hefty wench.

He saw her within five minutes. She was dancing with a tall man with a big Adam's apple and a skin condition. She looked bored. Glass caught her eye, winked and waved his drink in the air as an invitation. She winked back over the tall man's shoulder, a conspiratorial grin on her Pan-sticked face.

The dance ended.

"What is it?" said Glass as she excused herself from her partner and joined him at the bar.

"You're a smooth bugger, aren't you? I'll have a port and lemon please." Glass ordered the drink and paid for it with one of a wad of five pound notes which he extracted from his wallet. The gesture was not wasted on her.

"What's your name, then?"

"Walter," said Glass, who hated his name abbreviated.

"Mine's Eileen. Hello, Wally." She squeezed his hand and watched him slowly return his wallet to his inside pocket. He placed his hand on top of hers. This was not going to take him long. Her skirt was a good foot shorter than the current fashion, ending halfway up her thighs, and her Playtex sculptured breasts pointed through her jumper like twin models of the Pyramids. She finished the drink in ninety seconds.

"Another?" offered Glass. She agreed to be persuaded, and did not decline a further one five minutes later.

"Fancy a dance, Eileen?" There was a limit to his expense account.

" Why not."

He entwined himself around her on the dance floor, pressing his hips against hers and forcing his knee sensually between her legs. In turn, she brushed her bust against his chest and nibbled the lobe of his ear. Glass found this rather exhilarating, and coupled with the effect of the drink made him somewhat light-headed.

" The Leith police dismisseth us," he murmured.

" You what, luv?"

" Just testing if I'm drunk."

" Eh?"

" It's what the police used to make you say before they slung you in the cells. Before the breathaliser."

" Had much to do with the police, have you, Wally?"

" I've seen the inside of a few police stations in my time," admitted Glass truthfully.

" Bastards," opined Eileen. " Eh, Wally?"

" Too right," agreed the Inspector, feeling like Simon Peter. " Pigs."

Eileen tightened her arms around him and pressed herself against the lump in his trousers.

It was his pocket torch.

" I feel very randy, Wally. It must be the change."

" Yes." Glass was an authority on the manifestations of the menopause. Ever since he reached middle age, which in his case was shortly after his twenty-first birthday, he had been attracted to older women. Not for him the popular fantasies of young schoolgirls with hockey sticks or blonde-haired Swedish au-pairs. He preferred the unfastened hook of a liberty bodice or the sight of a pair of stays.

" Young women to me are like bromide," he once confessed to Sergeant Moon, who thought it extremely unlikely that young women would look at him anyway.

79

"Do you fancy coming to my place, Wally?" Beneath the scaffolding of corsetry, her appendix scar glowed as the blood raced round her veins in anticipation of carnal satisfaction.

The blood in Glass's veins stirred itself more slowly, rising from its usual resting-place at the soles of his feet.

"I'll ring for a taxi."

"Haven't you got a car, Wally? Just my luck. I never get fellas with cars."

In the taxi he slid his hand up the side of her leg and steered the conversation round to her gentleman friends. "You're not married then, Eileen?"

"Divorced. Ooh, that tickles, Wally."

"Live on your own, do you?"

"I have a flatmate, my friend Katie. She's divorced as well. But she won't be in cos she's staying with her fella in Millom for a few days. He works on the hovercrafts." She snuggled up to him. "So we'll be all alone."

Eileen lived at the back of the town near the railway, in a street of terraced boarding-houses whose heyday had been in the 1930s when trainloads of trippers arrived for Wake's Week. Now, many had been turned into flats.

The back bedroom was tiny, most of the room being taken up by a old brass bedstead that Glass knew would have fetched a fortune in the Portobello Road. The bed was roughly made and covered with a pink candlewick bedspread. He observed there were grease marks on one of the pillows.

"Are you getting in, Wally? It's a bit parky tonight." She had already relieved herself of her jumper.

Glass bent down to untie his shoelaces and his eye caught a pair of men's shoes sticking out from under the bed.

"She's got big feet, your flatmate," he said, holding one

under her nose.

" Oh!"

" Not very stylish either. I reckon these might fit me. Ten, eh? Big girl."

She paused in the act of unfastening the sixth clasp of her longline bra.

" Could be your brother, I suppose."

" All right, so I have a fella living with me from time to time. Not a crime, is it?" She undid the remaining hook and allowed her denuded bosom to tumble out and strike Glass in the stomach.

" So long as he's not here tonight."

She turned her attention to the skirt. " Don't worry, Wally. Patsy's away." She stepped out of the garment and threw it on the bed. " Till next weekend."

So it was Patsy. Glass smiled in self-congratulation as he struggled to insert his hand between her bulging flesh and the combined elasticity of her undergarments.

" Works out of town, does he?"

" Patsy doesn't work. Not if he can help it. No, he's gone to see his old Mum in Liverpool. He don't spend much time in Blackpool now."

" Liverpool, eh?" Bending his wrists backwards, Glass tightened his grip, gave an Olympic heave and succeeded in leavering the laddered tights, Aertex briefs and bikini pants past her knees in one swift movement.

" Know it, do you, Wally?"

His hands caressed her matted pubic hair. " I was there the other week watching the Rangers play at Everton."

Her hands crept to the waistband of his trousers and tried to sort out the various buttons which held up his braces and secured his fly.

" Whereabouts in Liverpool does he come from then?"

"Toxteth. Just past the Cathedral." She pulled his trousers to his knees to be greeted by the spectacle of his Thermal underwear.

"Not Stanhope Street?" He opened his knees, splitting the seam below his fly.

"No, Hill Street." She eyed him suspiciously, her hands lingering by his knees. "Why are you interested?"

He stepped out of his clothes, leaving his socks on because of the inclement weather, and pushed her gently onto the candlewick bedspread.

"I used to be in Liverpool in the war. I was in black-market butter in those days." His white bottom undulated unsteadily above her.

"Ooooooh, Wally, I thought that was your hand."

"He hasn't got any mates has he who might come round?"

"Oh, Wally, don't get so worried, course they won't. Anyway, he's only got one mate that I've ever seen and that's his brother."

Glass resumed his irregular thrusts.

"Ooooooh," she cried suddenly. "You didn't last long did you, Wally?"

Glass had got what he came for. There was no sense in hanging around. The next step was to find Patsy Kelly in Liverpool. "I'm sorry, Eileen," he sighed. "I'm afraid that is one of my shortcomings."

Sergeant Moon was asleep when Glass returned to the Imperial Hotel at half-past four, but he woke up soon enough when the Chief Inspector's shoes hit the floor one after the other.

"Sorry to wake you," apologised Glass happily, "but now that you *are* awake, you will be pleased to know that

I have traced one of the killers."

Moon was a person who did not wake easily. His first few moments of every day were invariably spent in somnivolent oblivion. Glass had disturbed him in the middle of a particularly pleasant dream where he and Ethel, strangely black in the dream, were winning the Mixed Doubles at Wimbledon using cricket bats instead of rackets.

Glass bent down to shake him. "Patsy Kelly is the boy's name. Tomorrow, or today rather," he looked guiltily at his watch, "we are going down to Liverpool to get him. "Can you hear me down there, Sergeant?"

"Yes, sir. Liverpool."

"Good. Well, you better get some sleep, Sergeant Moon. You've had a long day."

"Do we really know it's him, sir?" asked Moon, who was now beginning to wake up.

"I think it is and hunches are my speciality."

"Of course."

"Any news your end?"

"No, nothing. I only stayed on a couple of minutes downstairs after you left. Oh, there was one thing." Moon told him about The Executioner killing that he had heard of on the news.

"Well, well," whistled Glass. "So it wasn't a hoax. Debbings, eh? I remember the Highly case. In fact I was the one who dealt with it. He should have been hung in the first place."

"You sound pleased that he is dead."

"I'm delighted, Sergeant. And a most appropriate way for him to go as well."

"Do you think there will be any more killing, sir?"

"Bound to be, son. He'll be a hard one to catch. Not a job for schoolboys." Moon, aware of Glass's views on police college, let the reference to Detective Chief Inspector Knox pass. "And there will be more post office robberies, too, if we don't get hold of Patsy Kelly. We shall see the Blackpool police before lunch. I want a few enquiries made about his brother. And then we shall go over to Merseyside."

But they never made it because Glass's prophecy came true.

The second post office robbery took place just six hours later, whilst both men were still sleeping, at 10.30 p.m. on the morning of Saturday, March 13th, over 100 miles North, in Cumbria.

ELEVEN

Saturday, March 13th

Colonel Algernon Pavitt lived in reduced circumstances in Carlisle. During his career as a Defender of the British Empire in India, Europe and Africa, he never imagined he would end up in a bedsitting room with a shared kitchen and electric slot meter. But then, he never imagined either that Britain would give the Empire back again or that his inheritence, savings and investments would be rendered virtually worthless by inflation. He just knew that after a lifetime in the British Army he would probably have been better off if he had joined the SS.

Furthermore, he had had no more success with his marriage. The late Mrs. Pavitt had been a frail creature reared in the sublime air of Leamington Spa in the days when visitors came for the waters and most of the inhabitants were white. Certainly she had been too delicate a bloom to withstand the rigours of the Welfare State, and she had finally succumbed to Type AA influenza in the winter of '74.

The Colonel proved to be of stronger mettle. His posture remained erect, his voice still boomed like an angry bittern, and the long walks he took daily testified and probably contributed to his continuing good health.

He looked the part of the retired officer. His nose stretched out from his face like the bows of a ship, and his eyes shone like sapphires, encrusted deep in his suntanned, wrinkled skin which, from a distance, had the appearance of a chamois leather.

For recreation he read avidly all the weighty volumes of war memoirs that the local library could afford to buy, the verbose effusions of geriatric generals who all claimed to have won the war single-handed. In conversation with friends and strangers, he would often recount episodes from the books, inserting his own name in a suitable part of the narrative to emphasise his part in military history.

His standard of living was not high. The accumulated income from his Army pension, State pension and social security benefits was barely enough to keep him in a manner equivalent to that of his erstwhile African houseboy. Even the addition of a Disability pension for the loss of two minor fingers in India (burnt off, in fact, when a chip pan caught fire in the Officer's Mess) only enabled him to buy an extra ounce of tobacco a week.

Notwithstanding all this, Colonel Pavitt was a proud man and would, had the opportunity arisen, have died for his country. It was unlikely, however, that in the provincial backwaters of Cumbria, that any such opportunity would present itself.

He set out on his morning perambulation at nine-thirty. The day was clear and brisk, ideal walking weather. He circumnavigated the city walls past the Cathedral and Castle and back through the busy main street. Being Saturday, the Family Shopper was out in force.

He usually lunched at a small snack bar on the outskirts of town run by a fat widow called Mary. Here, for seventy-five pence, he could partake of a three-course meal rich in carbohydrates. A typical menu would be vegetable soup (powdered and watery), meat and two veg (usually cabbage and peas) and a solid suet pudding. The mashed potatoes were artificial.

On a Saturday morning, the Colonel's route extended to take in the post office near the snack bar where he would collect his various pensions.

On this particular Saturday at the same post office, he came closer to death than at any time since he held off the Germans single-handed in 1942.

The Hutchinson family had a smallholding fifteen miles from Carlisle in the middle of the Cumbrian farming country. It was not a big holding, just three acres, but enough to provide for Dick Hutchinson (47), his wife Jean (42) and their children Roger (12), Zita (11) and Gail (6).

Their main income was from poultry. Ten thousand day-old chicks were brought to them by the wholesalers and taken back six weeks later, unnaturally fattened for the table. The broiler system was not one that the family cared for, but it was the only one that paid.

They kept pigs (fifty Welsh/Landrace crosses), a goat (for milk), two horses (Zita was a keen rider, and rows of rosettes adorned her bedrom wall), a donkey (for grass cutting and company), a mixed assortment of interbred cats and a few free-range ducklings. Gail had been promised a pony of her own on her sixth birthday and her father had one in mind.

On the agricultural side they had an orchard which produced fruit and vegetables in such profusion as to be almost called a market garden.

On this particular Saturday Carlisle United were at home which meant Jean had to start her shopping early to be back to prepare lunch.

"Are you going with your Dad to the match?" she asked Roger.

"Naw. I'm going fishing with some lads from school."

"You're very fickle since they went out of the First Division," said Dick. "Anyway, I'm still going. Haven't missed a game yet. Dave Forshaw is picking me up at half-past one in his Land-Rover."

"Will you get me a thirty pence postal order while you are out, Mum?" asked Zita. "I want to send for these race cards of Arkle and Night Nurse."

"Okay, Zita. Come on, Gail, let's get you wrapped up, it's cold out."

"Can I take my doll's pram, Mummy?"

"Yes, of course." Jean put on her warm tweed coat and gathered her shopping-bag. She wrapped Gail in a fur-lined anorak with a pixie hood. Putting the doll's pram in the back of the Mini Clubman Estate, they set off along the country lanes towards Carlisle. The day was bright and clear although there was a strong breeze and the temperature was little above freezing. On the hedgerows, the first suspicion of spring buds gave the privets a veil of green and, in the fields, tiny lambs stretched their spindly legs.

Jean mentally ran over her shopping-list as she drove.

87

She wanted meat from the market, buttons for Gail's coat from Binns, food and underwear from Marks and Spencers, and she must not forget Zita's postal order.

Coming into the outskirts of the city she saw a post office. " I'm just going to get Zita's postal order, love, I shan't be a minute."

" Oh, can I come, too, Mummy," said Gail. " I want some sweets."

" All right."

It was a decision Jean Hutchinson would regret the rest of her life.

The Carlisle sub-post office was run by two Methodist ladies, the Misses Hough. One of the Misses Hough had, for a short period, been a Mrs. Spragg, but Mr. Spragg had been cursed with a rogue digestive system and, after a long series of encounters with scalpel-happy surgeons, he had finally died in agony in Chalfont St. Giles. There was no issue. Mrs. Spragg reverted to her maiden name and rejoined her spinster sister, Enid, at her business in Carlisle.

On Saturday mornings, it was the practice of Enid Hough to do the weekend shopping in town, leaving her sister to look after the post office. Saturday was never one of their busiest days. As in most towns, the shops on the outskirts tended to take more money on weekdays.

On this particular Saturday, Miss Alma Hough (nee Spragg) engaged herself between customers in the construction of a Balaclava helmet. At ten-thirty she put down her ball of steel-grey wool and was about to go into the back to make a cup of tea for herself when the bell rang and a lady came into the shop followed by a little girl holding a doll.

The lady smiled at Alma. " A thirty pence postal order,

"please."

"Certainly." Alma sorted through the money orders in the drawer. The lady was not anybody she knew.

"Can I have these, Mummy?" The little girl held up a small packet of Cadbury's Buttons. Alma thought she looked cute in her fur pixie hood.

The lady took the chocolates and put them on the counter. "How much will that be altogether?"

"Forty-six pence." The lady handed over a pound note, and Alma gave her the change.

"Thanks a lot," she said. "Cold this morning, isn't it?"

Alma agreed that indeed it was the coldest March she had known in years.

At this point everything started to happen. Two men dashed into the shop, brushing past the lady and her little girl as they turned away from the counter. The men stood menacingly in front of Alma Hough. She looked at their faces and saw they were wearing masks. She screamed.

At the precise moment that she screamed, as the lady customer and her small daughter turned round in horror, the door opened again and a man walked into the shop. He heard the scream and stopped.

"What's going on?" he shouted in a stentorian voice. Alma felt relief. It was Colonel Pavitt who came in every Saturday for his pension. Help was at hand. The Army was here.

But the colonel was not armed.

One of the men produced a gun. "Give me all the money in the till, woman." Alma recognised the masks—Yogi Bear and Barney Flintstone.

Colonel Pavitt took a step forward. The gunman turned round. "Nobody move or I shoot."

The little girl started to cry, and her mother put her

arms protectively round her. Alma's fingers trembled as she pulled notes from the till.

" Hurry up." There were not many notes. Only about fifty pounds that she used as a float.

Colonel Pavitt's voice rang out commandingly. " Give me that gun."

For an answer, the man jumped forward and grabbed hold of the little girl, dragging her away from her mother's grasp. He held the nozzle of the gun against her temple.

" Right. Anybody try to stop us and the kid gets it."

" The money," shouted his companion, and Alma thrust the notes through the division in the plastic screen. He grabbed them and both men moved down the shop.

" Out of my way, old man."

But Colonel Pavitt stood firm. He fixed the criminals with a rigid stare and held out his hand.

" You won't shoot, you scum."

It was the same mistaken assumption that cost Michael Spencer his life.

The gunman lifted the weapon from the child's head. " Move, I said."

Colonel Pavitt took another step forward. No more than three yards separated them. The masked man pointed the gun directly at his brain and slowly squeezed the trigger . . .

The explosion reverberated round the little shop, but Colonel Pavitt did not die.

His life was saved by a five-year-old girl.

Little Gail Hutchinson put her hand over the pistol and pushed it away. The bullet flew into the far wall of the shop.

Taking with it the little girl's hand.

Detective Chief Inspector Glass examined the morning

papers over a late breakfast at the Imperial Hotel in Blackpool.

The Megaphone carried banner headlines about The Executioner and his first victim.

"Timothy Slade has gone to town here," he commented. Sergeant Moon turned his attention from the *Daily Telegraph* where the story was second only to the latest British Leyland crisis.

"Just what The Executioner wants, isn't it? All this publicity."

Glass studied the article which occupied all of the front page and most of the second. "We know where *his* sympathies lie, anyway," he said, and Moon remembered the conversation with the reporter on the way to Leyton. "I like this bit. 'The Executioner is only doing the job that the Government, despite the people's wishes, has failed to do.' He is quite right too."

"A bit dangerous, don't you think," ventured the Sergeant, "a national newspaper virtually condoning a murder?"

"He goes on to say, 'Whilst we in no way condone this brutal crime . . .'"

"Mmmmmm," said Moon.

Glass turned his attention to the other pages. Queens Park Rangers were at home to Norwich. Should be good for two points, he thought. Norwich were in the relegation zone as usual. Red Rum was said to be in peak condition in his preparation for the Grand National, and readers were advised to back him now whilst the odds were still 12-1. Glass had already invested ten pounds at more favourable odds and smiled a smug grin. P. J. Proby was making another comeback after bankruptcy.

"I always thought he was a better singer than Tom

91

Jones," murmured the Chief Inspector aloud.

" Pardon," said Moon.

" P. J. Proby."

Moon looked blank. His musical tastes were confined to church choral and organ music, with a preference for Bach.

" Paging Detective Chief Inspector Glass. Please go to Reception. Detective Chief Inspector Glass to Reception, please." The Tannoy rang out throughout the hotel.

Glass rose creakingly to his feet. The gymnastics of the night before had taken their toll. At the desk he found Detective Inspector Moorcroft who greeted him with the intelligence of the Carlisle post office robbery.

" Come through to the restaurant," said Glass, " while I finish my breakfast and you can tell me all about it."

" Nothing much really to tell," said Moorcroft, taking a seat at the table. " We have arranged for a car to take you up to Carlisle. The journey should not take more than an hour and a half."

Glass poured himself another cup of tea from the large silver pot. " Any details of the robbery?"

" Apparently a customer was hurt. A little girl. Not seriously."

" Did they take much?"

" From all accounts it appears to have been a bit of a cock-up. Some people came into the shop, the men panicked and fled."

" The same men as before I take it?"

" Yogi Bear masks."

" It goes without saying," said Glass heavily, " that they vanished without trace."

" No report of any arrests so far."

" Another wasted journey ahead of us," whispered Glass

to Moon.

Inspector Moorcroft stroked his arboreal cheeks. " How did you get on with your enquiries last night? Anything to show?"

" A sore head and torn trousers," replied the Scotland Yard man.

" Really?"

" What do you know about a Patrick Kelly, known to his friends as Patsy."

" Patsy Kelly? One of the local hoodlums. We suspected him of being in on a couple of bank jobs, but nothing was proved. Vicious nature. Trained in Borstal."

" Ah," said Glass as if that explained everything.

" He's not been around for, let me see, must be at least twelve months. Word has it he was on the oil rigs. Don't believe it myself."

" No?"

" Too much like work."

" How about his brother?"

Moorcroft looked surprised. " I didn't know he had one."

" Reliable sources inform me," said Glass aphoristically, " that he had."

" You think Patsy Kelly might be mixed up in this?"

" Just a hunch," said Glass. " I'm famous for them." He drank the last of his tea. " We shall be five minutes packing. Is the car outside?"

" Yes. We might see you again then if you are looking for Kelly?"

" I don't think we shall find him here, but thanks for your help."

Fifteen minutes later they were on their way north, driving on the A586 towards Garstang to pick up the motorway at the A6/M6 junction one mile from the Forton services.

"You don't think we will find much in Carlisle then?" asked Moon.

"I shouldn't think so, but we will have to go. I *am* in charge of this case and it looks better if I turn up at the scene of the crime." Moon looked sharply at him. He was never quite sure when the Chief Inspector was being sarcastic. "No, my guess is that Patsy Kelly, if it is him, will be back in the Pool by now."

"Might it not be as well for us to alert the Liverpool police and have him picked up?"

"No direct evidence. We might frighten him off. No, I'll do it my way. I know where to find him."

"Oh, you do?" said Moon wistfully. The Chief Inspector had a tendency to conduct his cases in secret, making his subordinates feel rather superfluous. There was little chance for him to shine as a Great Detective when half the time he did not know what was going on.

They arrived in Carlisle shortly before two, by which time the second Miss Hough had returned to calm her sister; Colonel Pavitt had returned to his bedsitting room, promising to be available for later questioning, and Gail Hutchinson had been rushed to Carlisle City General Hospital for an emergency operation on her hand, her mother accompanying her.

Nobody had seen the car in which the two robbers had made their escape. Indeed, there was even conjecture that they had not used a vehicle at all but had merely mingled on foot with the Saturday shoppers and melted anonymously into the crowds. Colonel Pavitt, the only person in the post office who might reasonably be expected to give chase, had been too preoccupied, along with the girl's mother and Miss Hough, in attending to little Gail.

Having obtained details of the robbery from the local police station, the Scotland Yard men set out to inspect the latest group of witnesses, and already Sergeant Moon was beginning to agree with his superior's opinion about the value of the trip.

The Misses Hough were still in a state of mild hysteria after the major disruption to their genteel, ordered existence.

Previously, their lives had revolved round bridge parties, church sermons, knitting patterns, winter vests, Brasso, Thermogen and Gilbert and Sullivan. The real world had never intruded. Even the once-married Miss Hough exuded a primness that suggested the carnal obligations of the union had proved distasteful to her.

Equally distasteful was the questioning by the big Chief Inspector from Scotland Yard. Glass had no time for whinnying. He wanted answers and took no notice of the jar of sal volatile placed strategically within reach of Miss Hough's trembling stalk-like fingers.

" You cannot describe them at all?"

Her thin frame shook as more tears cascaded like a leaking cistern down her skin-stretched cheeks. No. Other than they wore masks, she could not describe them.

" God will punish them," stated her sister piously, but Glass could not wait for God. Colonel Pavitt seemed a more likely person to help him.

They found the Colonel in his bedsitting room enjoying a frugal tea of wholemeal bread and Cheddar cheese. A coal effect electric fire in the tiled grate was unlit although the room was chilly.

" That little girl saved my life," he said emotionally, " but what a price to pay. My God, it doesn't bear thinking about." He saw Glass shiver. " Can only afford to put the

95

fire on in the evenings. Pension and all that." Moon observed a half-empty flask of brandy on the sideboard and concluded that the Colonel preferred to invest his meagre pittance in inner warmth.

The Colonel went on to apologize for his failure to capture the men single-handed, despite his skill in unarmed combat. He also regretted that his normally keen powers of observation had failed him and he could not describe either of his antagonists.

"You have nothing to be ashamed of," said Glass sincerely. "You did stand up to them which is more than one in a thousand people would." He did not add that only one in a thousand would be so completely witless as to challenge a man with a loaded gun; possibly because he knew that he himself would probably have done the same thing. Blind rage was a strong motivator.

Their next call was at the hospital. Gail Hutchinson was detained in the children's ward.

"Nothing we could do to save the hand," the surgeon told Glass. "The tendons were severed and the bones fragmented." Glass experienced the cold fury he had felt when he looked at Michael Spencer's body. He wanted nothing more than to be given five minutes alone with the killers. Once again his mind turned to The Executioner, and he wondered if *he* had witnessed a scene like this and if that was why he had started his campaign of revenge.

"Can I have a word with her?" he asked the surgeon.

"She is under sedation," interposed the Ward Sister, "and fast asleep."

"She has lost a lot of blood, you know," explained the surgeon, "and she is suffering from shock."

"Tomorrow?"

"Call back in the morning and we shall see. I am making

no promises."

"We'll go and see the family," said Glass to Moon. "I take it her mother has gone home."

"Just before you arrived. Both her parents were here." The sister's voice softened. "I hope to God you catch them," she said in her lilting Irish brogue. "They are animals who would do that to a little girl."

Glass agreed, and they left for the Hutchinsons' small-holding. The mountains loomed menacingly from the shadows, black and bereaved in the darkness of approaching night. A sharp wind rustled the bare branches of the trees, and somewhere, behind a barn, an owl hooted. Glass lit a Craven A and puffed furiously until a thick fug filled the car. "I can't get used to this fresh air," he explained.

The Hutchinsons' cottage looked pictuesque by night, the carriage lamp outside the solid oak door lighting up the whitewashed walls and outlining the moving shapes of the apple trees in the adjoining orchard. The living-room was warm and cosy. A log fire burned in the grate and a smell of meat cooking wafted in from the kitchen.

"If I could get my hands on them," said Dick Hutchinson. He stood against the mantelpiece, almost as tall as the low, beamed ceiling.

Jean Hutchinson sat in a big armchair beside the fire, a cup of hot, sweet tea on her knee. Two extra mugs were brought in for the detectives.

"Sugar is on the table," indicated Zita who seemed to have taken over the domestic duties. "I'm going outside to help Roger feed the horses."

Jean Hutchinson sipped her tea. "We were going to buy Gail a pony for her birthday next month."

Glass did not reply. What could he say? Pony riding did not come easy with only one hand.

" You have been to see her?" asked Dick Hutchinson.

" In the morning. I take it you will both be there."

" We are going first thing. The children are looking after the farm."

" Another happy family with their life in ruins," said Glass as they drove back to Carlisle. " All for fifty pounds. And so unnecessary."

" It could have been worse," said Moon. " At least she is still alive."

" Even so . . ." Glass took out the familiar red packet and his box of Swan matches. " First that Spencer kid loses her father and now this one gets her hand shot off. All innocent people."

" There can't be much planning to these jobs," said Sergeant Moon thoughtfully. " I mean, small post offices, no large amounts of cash."

" But virtually unguarded and easy to rob."

" And why Leyton one day and then Carlisle. And the car found in Blackpool. What is the connection?"

" That is what we have to find out. In the meantime, we book into an hotel, have some dinner, and then an early night. We could do with the rest and there is nothing we can do now until tomorrow when we see the child."

" And then?"

" And then, Sergeant Moon, we go back down the M6. First thing Monday morning we take our trip to Liverpool. I have a feeling that a chat with Patsy Kelly might help answer your questions."

TWELVE

For Detective Chief Inspector Robin Knox, the day ahead promised nothing but hard slog. The pressure was on him to find some clue as to the identity of The Executioner.

But it was with a light-hearted tread that he skipped down the steps in answer to Sergeant Evans' ringing at his door-bell. His night with Sue Owen had been something rather special, even for a man used to the company of the most beautiful women in Society.

" I think I have fallen in love, Evans," he greeted his assistant.

" I don't believe it, sir. Not you. Here, have an Aspirin. You will soon get over it. When are you seeing her again?"

" She has gone off to the Lakes for the weekend with that *Megaphone* reporter, Timothy Slade. I am seeing her on Monday night."

" Not the best start to your big love affair," opined Sergeant Evans gloomily. " Spending the weekend with another bloke."

" She's known him ages and it was already planned."

" Bit of a dandy, this Slade, from all accounts."

Knox gritted his teeth. " I'd rather talk about The Executioner."

" Of course." Evans recognised the banter was over. " What is the plan of campaign, sir?"

" We see all the prisoners who had much to do with Debbings and find out if he said anything to suggest that he expected trouble when he came out."

" And if he didn't?"

" Then it is back to the files. We make a list of all the men, and women, who would have been hanged since the death penalty ended."

" But there must be hundreds of them. And even suppose we are on the right track, we don't know which one he will pick next. We can't act as nursemaid to them all."

" We can talk to as many as possible. Perhaps find a common denominator."

The Governor of Wormwood Scrubs took a similar hopeless view. " If it is a personal revenge motive, it will stop at Debbings. If not, then the man is homicidal and it is anybody's guess." He sat behind a leather-topped desk in an office covered on three walls by books. From a pipe-rack next to his blotter he selected a curved briar, filled it with aromatic tobacco from a plastic pouch and applied a match to the bowl. " The two men you need to see are Mullings and Skoyles, both lifers. They worked in the wash-house with Debbings and both shared a cell with him at one time or another. When they were not in solitary." He rang an extension on his telephone. " I'll have them brought up."

Mullings was a short man with a bull neck which made his head look as if it was sinking into his body like in quicksands. A flattened nose gave him a peculiarly bovine expression, emphasised by beady, puffy eyes.

" Mullings, this is Detective Chief Inspector Knox from Scotland Yard. He wishes to ask you a few questions about Alfred Debbings."

The prisoner sniffed and wiped his nose with the back of his hand. Small clumps of hair protruded from his nostrils in such profusion that Knox thought they would interest the Bonsai Society.

"I never liked the bastard," he said in a toneless voice. "He was a moody fucker. Couldn't get a word out of him most days. Any road, I've no time for sods like him what put the boot in an old fella."

Knox pointed out that Mullings himself was incarcerated for first-degree murder.

"That were different. You come home and find some bastard stuck up your wife and see what you'd frigging do."

Knox winced at the inelegant vocabulary and refrained from mentioning Mullings' three previous convictions for grievous bodily harm. Instead he asked, "As far as you know, did he have any enemies?"

"No one could stand the bastard."

"Yes, quite, but can you think of anyone who hated him enough to go out of their way to kill him?"

A deep furrow appeared on Mullings' brow. He was thinking and the process seemed to cause him pain. "No," he said at last. "Who'd be bothered?"

"That seems to sum Debbings up," said Sergeant Evans.

"Not very helpful," agreed the Governor when Mullings had been taken back to the cells. "Odd how they have their own code of ethics. We have Trevellyn in here at the moment."

"The Old Bailey Trial last week?"

"That's the one. Murdered a pensioner for his weekly fifteen quid, bit of a sadist they say."

"Laughed at the judge when he only got seven years according to the papers," said Evans.

"Well, he is not laughing now. The men are giving him a hard time down there. We have had to put him in solitary twice for his own safety."

The second prisoner was shown in. Arnold 'Sonny' Skoyles was a lanky man with a bald, turnip-shaped head that would have made an excellent Hallowe'en lantern. He was serving a life sentence for manslaughter, the outcome of a gangland fracas in a public house in Shoreditch one autumn night when Frank The Greek received a six-inch blade straight through his Adam's apple.

"Sit down, Skoyles. This is Detective Chief Inspector Knox from Scotland Yard."

"I know who that is, guvnor, he put me in here. How's the Sweeney then, Mr. Knox?" Knox inclined his head gracefully. "No hard feelings, guv. It was a fair cop."

"True enough," said the Chief Inspector. "We want your help, Sonny, on this Debbings murder."

"Well, that was nothing to do with me, was it? I mean, I'm stuck in here."

"You shared a cell, so presumably you were quite friendly. He may have told you something."

"Not my friend, guv. Don't get me wrong, we never fell out. He just kept himself to himself. Wasn't one of the boys, if you know what I mean."

"So it would be unlikely that any of 'the boys' had it in for him?"

"No way. I suppose he might have crossed one of his fences, but he didn't seem the type, did he?" Skoyles looked scornful. "I mean, he was hardly big league. He only did that old geezer cos he lost his bottle when he got pinched." He lowered his voice confidentially. "Here, guv, is it true that The Executioner has done for him?" Knox nodded. "Christ, we'll all be up Shit Creek then. I'm getting back to my cell before he comes for me. I'm out in three years, Mr. Knox. Try and catch him before then, will you?"

" A dead end, it would appear," said the Governor as Skoyles was returned gratefully to his cell.

" It is back to the files, I fear," said Knox. " You could help me here, sir. I am compiling a list of murderers convicted since 1955 when the death penalty was abolished. Many of them will have been released from prison by now. Perhaps you could let me have records of men from this jail."

" I see to it right away, Chief Inspector."

" Thank you, Mr. O'Brien?"

" Back to the Yard, sir?" asked Sergeant Evans as they drove away from the grim prison.

" Yes. Maybe some information will have come in. The last trace we have of Debbings is at 4.30 when he went into the Classic Cinema. We do not know what time he came out or where he went. Our big hope is that somebody saw him in the company of The Executioner. I cannot believe he would be wandering in St. James's Park on his own."

" Well, the men are going the rounds with his photograph, sir. They could come up with something. He had seen both films at the cinema by eight o'clock so it is an even bet that he spent the night in Soho."

" You mean the evening, Sergeant. He spent the *night* swinging from a tree in St. James's Park."

Sergeant Evans stood corrected. " I reckon a club maybe or perhaps a prostitute. After all that time in jail, sir."

" He may have lost the taste for it, Sergeant."

" After three hours of ' Sexy Lovers ', sir, it might have come back to him."

" Well, we shall have to wait and see. In the meantime, there is all this paperwork to go through. Not an exciting weekend for us." He thought of Sue, up in the Lakes with Timothy Slade. " You know, Evans, sometimes I wonder if I am not in the wrong job. Perhaps I should have been a journalist."

" Sir?"

" Have you ever been in love, Evans?"

" In 1961, sir. With Mrs. Evans. He blushed fetchingly, " The wife, sir."

" I do know who Mrs. Evans is, Sergeant." He looked wistfully north to where he imagined Windermere to be. " I think I will take that Aspirin after all."

THIRTEEN

Sunday, March 14th

Sue Owen was up early after her night at Robin Knox's flat, no mean achievement as she had arrived home only shortly before the milkman. But she had arranged to go to the Lakes for the weekend with her friend and sometime suitor, Timothy Slade.

" I want to make a little detour on the way," the reporter told her as they sped up the M6 in his orange Audi 100GL. " There has been another Post Office robbery, in Carlisle."

" Oh yes? Isn't that the case Detective Chief Inspector Glass is on?"

Slade looked surprised. " Fancy you knowing that. You never told me you were acquainted with Scotland Yard officers."

" Like Robin Knox you mean?"

" He is dealing with The Executioner case." He told her

about the letter to *The Times* and Debbings' murder.

"So that was why he was chasing about last night. We just had a few drinks," she added coquettishly as she observed Tim's startled expression.

They reached Carlisle by six, just too late to catch Glass at the hospital or to see Gail Hutchinson who was sleeping.

"We'll try the witnesses," said Slade. "You take the notebook and say you are my assistant." They found the Post Office where The Misses Hough had recovered from their hysteria and were delighted to pose for photos for *The Megaphone*. "Wonderful sob stuff," whispered Tim. "'Lonely spinster faces masked killer.' What a headline. Can you try to get the Bible in as well." Colonel Pavitt was photographed beside his collection of war books, wearing his medal. "'Elderly war hero in suburban gun battle,'" enthused Tim. "Right, we'll send this film Red Star to Euston then get to the hotel." They were staying at the Salutation at Ambleside. "I'll come back in the morning while you have a lie-in."

At one time she would have insisted on going with him, but this was not like other weekends she had spent with the reporter. This time she felt strangely guilty and she knew the reason was that she had met Robin Knox.

FOURTEEN

Detective Chief Inspector Glass and Sergeant Moon spent the night at the Cumbrian Hotel beside Carlisle Station. They enjoyed an excellent dinner (Moon had the rump steak whilst Glass treated himself to the fresh salmon at the taxpayers' expense) and eight hours' uninterrupted sleep.

Soon after breakfast on Sunday morning they presented themselves at the City General Hospital to see Gail Hutchinson.

" Can you wait half an hour?" asked the sister, and was told they could wait all day if necessary."

" Is there anywhere we can get a cup of tea?" added Glass.

" Only the public waiting-room I'm afraid."

" We're not proud. Come on, Sergeant."

The tea was brewed in a giant silver urn and served in thick white cups. Each customer received a free rich tea biscuit courtesy of the WVS.

" I'd like mine strong, please," instructed the Chief Inspector. " The colour of an African woman."

" We have plenty of those here," smiled the tea lady, sociably. " Would your friend like his the same or would he prefer an English woman?"

Glass looked across sceptically at Moon. " Weak and insipid, I think." He carried the cups to the table where Moon was engrossed in a four-year old copy of *Woman's Own*.

" Enjoying it, Sergeant?" he asked. Moon coloured. Glass picked up a five-year-old copy of *Woman* and turned to the problem page.

" Well, well, Chief Inspector Glass. Fancy meeting you here. I couldn't have timed it better." The two detectives looked up to see Timothy Slade come striding into the waiting-room.

" Hello, Tim, you're a day late. The robbery was yesterday."

" I was here yesterday, just missed you. They told me to

come back today." He nodded cordially to Sergeant Moon. "Any developments?"

"If you mean have we caught anybody, no. We are, as they say, continuing our enquiries."

"Any chance of a quick photo of the little girl?" He produced a Minox camera from his jacket pocket.

"I don't mind." Glass looked around. "What happened to all your rivals?"

"It is a long way to Carlisle. They rely on the local agencies, and most of them were happy with what they got yesterday—interview with the parents, school photo of the kiddie, statement from Detective Chief Inspector Glass who said the police were following a definite line of enquiry."

"Mmmm. So why are you still here?"

"Would you believe I am on holiday? We are staying at the Salutation at Ambleside for the weekend."

"Who is the ' we '?"

"A lady of my acquaintance," smiled Timothy Slade.

"Hang on a minute. Ambleside is fifty miles from here."

"Let us say I have a personal interest in this case, after Leyton. Besides, good reporters like to be where the action is." He pointed to their tea cups. "Do you want another?" Both policemen shook their heads. Slade went over to the counter and Glass returned to Evelyn Home.

"Do you think it will be long before we can see her? I left my lady back at the hotel." Timothy returned to sit beside them and dipped his rich tea biscuit into his cup.

"Another twenty minutes," said Glass.

But the sister appeared only ten minutes later to conduct them all to Gail Hutchinson's ward. Gail's parents were already with her. Glass smiled engagingly and introduced Timothy Slade as a minor Cecil Beaton who had just come along for the ride, thus enabling him to take his photographs without commotion.

"Now then," said Glass gently, sitting on the end of the child's bed. "What did you notice about those nasty men?"

Far from being reticent Gail was eager to talk. "One of them looked like Yogi Bear and he tried to shoot that old man, but I stopped him, didn't I?"

"You certainly did." But at what a price, he thought, and was glad he did not have to break the news to her about her hand. "Did you notice anything else about him apart from him looking like Yogi Bear?"

"He had a picture on his arm."

"A picture? The detective's voice rose in anticipation.

"In blue ink. Of a flower."

"Which arm was that on?"

"The one with the gun."

"Was that the left or the right?"

She giggled and shook her head. "I don't know," and she put both little arms in front of her and looked from one to the other in confusion.

"O.K. You did very well to notice that. Was there anything else you can think of?"

There was not. Timothy took his pictures, Glass thanked the little girl and exchanged more words of commiseration with her parents and they walked out of the hospital.

"It is the first positive item of identification," said Glass. "Strange how children notice things that adults miss."

"It is a bloody shame for that kiddie," said Timothy vehemently. "And when you catch them they will probably just get seven years like Trevellyn. Doesn't it make you mad?"

"Well, you know what I think, Tim, the same as you. I

see in some part of Saudi Arabia they have gone back to Islam law because the English system did not work. They chop their hands off for theft now." He shook his head sadly. " I can't see it coming in here."

" Are you going straight back to London?"

Glass shot Moon a warning look. " Just one or two things to do up here, then we shall be."

" Well, I am off to Ambleside. I shall be back in town tomorrow so I will ring you at the Yard in case you have any news."

" You are keeping very quiet about Liverpool," commented Moon as they watched the reporter's Audi disappear down the road.

" Nothing to be gained in opening our mouths yet. He will be the first to know when we have anything concrete. He did us proud on the Leyton story."

" That's true. So when do we leave for Liverpool?"

" Tomorrow. We will catch the first Glasgow-Liverpool express that stops at Carlisle. I do not think that another night at the Cumbrian would come amiss. I was rather partial to that fresh salmon."

It was when they got back to the Cumbrian that they heard the news. That morning the *Sunday Times* had carried a copy of a new letter from The Executioner.

Detective Chief Inspector Knox was summoned to the office of the Assistant Commissioner of Scotland Yard late on the Saturday afternoon where he was shown the original of the letter which had arrived by post at the office of the *Sunday Times*.

The letter read :

Dear Sir,

You will now be aware that my previous letter was not a hoax. My intentions, as detailed hitherto, have not altered. Alfred George Debbings is only my first victim. You may expect the second within the week. Innocent people need not be afraid. I do not kill for gain but to set an example. Only the guilty will die.

By the hand of . . .
THE EXECUTIONER.

"Well," demanded the Assistant Commissioner, "have you no lead on this Debbings murder yet?"

"None at all, sir. The only pieces of evidence we have had are the card he left behind, the rope round the dead man's neck and the typing paper, the Croxley Script again."

"What about the printing on the card?"

"We discovered the logo was not, in fact, printed. Just cleverly drawn in Indian ink."

"And the typewriter?"

"An Imperial like a thousand others."

"So what line are you working on now?"

"As I see it, sir, there are two ways we can approach this case, and I am working on both. One is to trace The Executioner on the evidence we have."

"Which is nothing."

"Precisely. The second way is to anticipate his next victim. To this end I am going through all the records to find out the men, and women, who have escaped the death penalty since it was abolished. If we can take his letter literally, we can forget murders of revenge, husbands killing their wives' lovers, that sort of thing; and I think that underworld murders can be discounted. I am working on the theory that he is only after men who have killed innocent victims, perhaps people disassociated from the main crime like eye witnesses or bystanders."

"And then what? We have not got the men to act as nursemaids to a bunch of murderers."

"There won't be that many. A lot will still be in prison, some will have emigrated or died. Besides, it will not be for a long period, seven days at the most if what the letter says is true."

The Assistant Commissioner nodded. "All right. The men will be made available. I do not like the way this case is going, Robin. Too much public sympathy for the criminal. Have you seen these?" He held up a bunch of newspapers. "A Tory M.P. has tabled a motion for the return of hanging. An Essex housewife has started a campaign to reinstate the birch in schools. The mood is veering towards anarchy, and Scotland Yard is coming in for a lot of criticism. These Post Office robberies don't help. Two within four days, a policeman shot dead and no sign of criminals brought to justice."

"I would say that The Executioner is potentially more dangerous than them if only for the precedent he might set."

"I agree. And he is trading on a heavy backlash of public opinion after the so-called soft methods of recent years. We must catch him before the response to his methods becomes something more than letters to the newspapers. Before other people start reaping revenge themselves. Remember, once the system of law and order breaks down, the country becomes ripe for takeover by subversive groups."

The interview was concluded. Knox found Sergeant Evans and they spent the rest of the day going through the records.

Sunday brought reports from the two officers who had been taking Debbings' photo round Soho in the hope of finding someone who had seen him during his last hours on earth. But they had drawn a blank.

"Little point in continuing now, Turner," said Knox. "I shall be wanting you and Cohen for a different job. Bodyguard work."

He joined Evans in the canteen for lunch. "Lamb and greens," complained the Sergeant. "We were having roast chicken at home. Why is it always us who works Sundays?"

Knox ignored the question. "How many men have we got on your list?"

"Nineteen, sir."

"And we have got twenty-one on mine. That is forty men we need, Sergeant."

"Will we get them, sir?"

"With the blessing of the Chief. It is the only chance we have of catching him. Remember, there is no personal motive involved in these killings, he will be a stranger to his victims and he is too clever to leave any traces behind him. We have got to get him on the job"

"Will we be warning the men that we are guarding?"

"No. It will only make them edgy, they may vary their routine and we might scare him off. No, we just watch and wait, and we should not have to wait too long. Today is Sunday. There are six days left to his deadline."

FIFTEEN

Monday, March 15th

The Glasgow-Euston Inter-City express drew into Carlisle Station at 9.17 a.m., just twelve minutes late. " Almost on time today," grumbled one sarcastic regular to Glass, but the Chief Inspector was in a benign mood. The night at the Cumbrian Hotel, with more fresh salmon and rump steak, had been exceedingly cordial, and now he was on his way to solve the Post Office Robberies Case single-handed.

They changed trains at Preston and arrived at Liverpool Lime Street dead on time at 11.20 a.m. " We will use the Adelphi for our base," said Glass. " It is as near as any-where.

The Adelphi Hotel, a few yards down the road in Lime Street, had the hallowed atmosphere of a Victorian railway terminus. Glass organised a double room and spent the next half hour making telephone calls. One of them was to Detective Superintendent Snow of the Liverpool C.I.D. who arranged to call and see him after lunch. They had a snack in the Zodiac Coffee Bar which was part of the hotel, then returned to their room where Glass made more phone calls.

Superintendent Snow turned up half an hour later. He was a smart-looking man with an athletic gait which belied his forty-seven years. His hair was silver grey but still thick and wavy, and his smile and easy charm bore more than a passing resemblance to a young Cary Grant.

" Pleased to meet you, Chief Inspector. Let us dispense with the formalities, shall we? Tony is the name."

" Walter," said Glass. " And this is Sergeant Moon." The two shook hands. Glass picked up the phone and ordered drinks from Room Service. " I take it whisky will be acceptable?"

" Oh yes, excellent," said Tony Snow, and Sergeant Moon agreed on the off chance that he might be offered one. Glass ordered his usual Southern Comfort for himself.

" Right. Let me tell you why we are here. Cigarette?" He handed across the red packet of Craven A and the Liverpool detective took one. Glass provided the matches, then proceeded to outline their progress on the case to date.

" And you think Kelly could be your man?" said Tony Snow when the narrative ended.

" No evidence, but I get these hunches. Now the information that I have is that he is living with his old mother in Hill Street, but I have checked in the Directory and there is no mention of a Kelly there."

" Must be the only street in Liverpool without one. Leave it to me and I'll ask around. I have a few contacts who could be useful."

The drinks arrived and Glass did the honours.

" If you do find him, what then?" asked Snow. " Shall you want our help?"

" Yes and no. I can't just walk in and arrest him. No evidence." Moon breathed a sigh of relief. He had feared that the Chief Inspector would march in with handcuffs in one hand and truncheon in the other and do just that. " Initially, I just want to talk to him, but in case he tries to run for it I would like a couple of your men on the spot."

"No problem. I'll ring you at the hotel later then, Walter, with all the information that you want."

"This could be it, Sergeant," said Glass, when the Liverpool man had gone. "We shall soon know if my little hunch is right."

The call from Detective Superintendent Snow came at ten to nine. "I have not got the address you want I'm afraid. His mother does live at Hill Street, but he has left and nobody seems to know where he is, least of all his old Ma. She is half deaf, half blind and half pissed."

"Oh," said Glass despondently.

"However," continued Snow, "I can tell you that he is still living in the area, we think possibly with a prostitute called Chinese Jill. You will find her in any of the clubs around Upper Parliament St., the Yaruba, the Nigeria, the All Nations or, most likely, the Afrikaana. But be careful how you go up there. It is like Harlem at night, and white men are as popular as Hitler at a Bar Mitzvah."

"Thanks for the tip."

"I will have a car-load of men at your disposal standing by all night. As soon as you need me ring this number." Glass wrote the digits on the back of his Craven A packet. "You will get straight through to me there. Best of luck, Walter."

"It's on," Glass shouted to Moon with elation. "This could be the last lap. Now I want you to go up to the room and stay there until I phone, which will be as soon as I find the address. Right?" Moon nodded. He was used to being left behind.

"You are sure you don't want me to come?" he said half-heartedly.

"I am less conspicuous on my own," repeated Glass. "Don't worry. You'll hear from me soon enough."

A taxi picked up the Chief Inspector at nine-thirty and conveyed him to Liverpool 8. They drove along Berry Street, through the Chinese quarter of the city, and into Upper Parliament Street which cut across the borders of Toxteth and Dingle. On the one side, derelict terraced slums and overcrowded tenements ran down to the murky waters of the Mersey, and on the other, once elegant Georgian mansions had deteriorated into ghettoes for deprived blacks, courtesy of Liverpool Corporation who preferred to erect ugly new concrete blocks rather than restore the fine old buildings.

" Anywhere special you wanna be dropped, ace?" They had reached the top of Upper Parliament Street, and Glass had still not picked out the Afrikaana.

" Drive down again and drop me by the Cathedral." The Anglican Cathedral, started in 1903 and now almost finished, towered over the area in Gothic grandeur, dwarfing even the classical four storey houses on its perimeter.

Glass alighted from the vehicle and started to walk back up the hill away from the docks, peering sharply into each doorway until, at last, he found what he was lookng for.

The Afrikaana did not go out of its way to attract passing custom. Puce paint peeled from the stone walls, half the neon sign over the door was unlit, and no posters adorned the building to suggest that entertainment or merriment of any description might be found within.

Glass pressed the red button at the side of the door. It swung open slowly and he observed that it was lined with steel.

" Yo' member, suh?" A small fat man holding the door knob posed the question. He had a brown skin dotted at intervals with black warts like currants in a wholemeal scone. He stood behind a wooden counter which framed the entrance.

"Yeah," breathed Glass, trying out his new Kojak impression to suitable effect. A pound note changed hands and a wooden flap in the counter was raised to permit his entry. Four large men, also brown but without the warts, stood aside from the barricade to let him pass.

The hallway of the club had been little altered from the days when it was a private dwelling-house. In one front room a game of billiards was in progress, and in the other a few old men sat reading newspapers or watching a monochrome TV set in the corner. Pinned to a notice board beside a wide staircase were lists of sports teams, darts matches, community events and political messages. It was very like a Y.M.C.A. except that Glass was the only white man to be seen.

"Yo' coat, suh?" A West Indian girl shouted at his elbow from a recess in the wall at the top of some stone stairs. He parted with the shapeless garment wordlessly and followed the sound of music to the basement. A steel band was performing at the far end of the club, perched precariously on a stage constructed from upturned beer crates. Glass made his way round the periphery of the dance floor which was crammed with writhing couples. They danced in a series of orgasmic pelvic thrusts which interested Glass who thought he might introduce it at the Compton Road Welfare and Social Club.

"Do you wanna dance?" The invitation came from a Chinese girl who looked all of fifteen and was quite pretty. Glass exhaled a cloud of smoke and permitted her to lead him onto the dance floor.

"Looking for a girl are you, luv?" Her voice had a thick Scouse accent.

"I might be. How much?"

" Twenty quid."

" What's your name?"

" Jill." He could hardly believe his good fortune. So soon. Things were going well.

" It's a bit dear, isn't it?"

" You don't know until you've tried it, do you, mister?" She pulled her hair into bunches round her ears which made her look even more prepubescent. " Do you like schoolgirls? I've got plaits at home." All this was whispered into Glass's ear in a low voice that would have driven other men wild with desire. Unfortunately, Glass preferred grandmothers to schoolgirls and remained impassive.

" I'll give you ten," he offered, " but I want some information." Her face clouded, showing a sudden fear which did not need a Scotland Yard detective to recognise as guilt.

" Here, you're not the fuzz, are you?"

" You're joking."

" What do you want from me, then?"

" I'm looking for someone. I heard he was a friend of yours."

" Who is he?"

" Fella called Patsy Kelly."

More fear in her face. " Sure you're not the fuzz?"

" Course I am."

" What about him then? Not saying I know him, mind."

" *Is* he a friend of yours?" persisted Glass.

" He was. He ain't now. Ripped me off good and proper he did."

" Well, you'll be pleased to know that some of the boys ain't too happy with him either. You know where he might be?"

" Cost you fifteen notes, mister."

" I said ten."

" Fifteen." The narrow eyes looked into his and her knee rubbed softly into his groin.

" I could buy a *Kelly's Directory* for fifteen. Ten."

She took the two five pound notes that appeared as if by magic in his hand.

" All right, sod yer. Jermyn St. First house. He lives in the basement. And I hope you get the bastard."

" Thank you, Jill." They stopped dancing, and Glass made as if to leave. She held on to his arm.

" Hey," she said. " Don't you want a jump then?"

Glass shuddered. " Not on a full stomach." In the finest manner of Sunday newspaper reporters, he made his excuses and went in search of a public telephone. He found one next to the Gents. He dialled the Adelphi Hotel and asked for Moon's room.

" We're on," he said in a low voice. " Get a taxi down here. I'm at the Afrikaana Club in Upper Parliament Street. Be here in fifteen minutes."

He put the phone down and dialled again, Tony Snow's private line.

" Walter here, Tony. Are you set?" He gave him the address. " Basement flat. I am going in through the front so hang around the back in case there is another way out. Give it half an hour from now."

He lit a Craven A and returned to the club. Jill was now back on the floor dancing with an obese octoroon. He ordered a Southern Comfort and sat on a stool at the bar. An ageing crone took the seat next to him. She smelt of sweat, and her mouth, which was open to facilitate her breathing, housed only one tooth. " Buy a lady a drink, sailor," she wheezed, and the tooth wiggled in its mooring.

Glass handed over a fifty pence. " Buy a bar of soap with

the change."

"Piss off, you fairy," she cried, but he had downed his drink and gone.

He was waiting on the pavement when the taxi bearing Sergeant Moon pulled up outside the club. He jumped into the back seat and leaned through the partition to re-direct the driver to their new destination.

"This is it," he said to Moon. The last lap. Tony Snow's men are on their way."

The car turned into Princes Drive, past the National Westminster Drive-in Bank, the first one of its kind in Britain. On either side of the tree-lined dual carriageway stood more huge Victorian houses, most of them converted into bedsits and flats for students from the nearby University, but still retaining their grandeur.

"It won't be long before those are down," commented Glass. "Not the best of areas, is it?"

"This is where the Mersey Poets lived, Liverpool 8," said Moon. "You know, Roger McGough, Brian Patten and Adrian Henri. There was a big art movement here at the time of the Beatles. Haven't you heard of Arthur Dooley, the sculptor?"

Glass looked at him balefully. "Sometimes, Moon, I wonder if you are cut out to be a policeman. Perhaps something more artistic would have been better for you. A ballet dancer maybe. Or something connected with butterflies."

Moon said nothing. He had always considered Glass to be a man of philistine tastes.

"Jermyn Street coming up, blue."

"Drive past, will you, and stop us at the next corner," The driver glided to the roundabout in front of Princes Park and they disembarked outside the wrought iron gates.

"We'll walk across," said Glass. "The exercise will do

you good."

Two girls were walking slowly in front of them, obviously engaged in the kerbside crawling trade. The two detectives crossed over.

"Keep with me all the time," warned Glass. They reached the house. Glass went up the path first and rang the bell. It was a semi-detached house of two storeys but with a skylight in the roof which indicated an attic. A light came on in the hall and the shadow of a woman came closer to the frosted glass front door.

"Hello, luv," said Glass in a rough voice. "Is Patsy in?"

She was in her late twenties. Her make-up was caked, her nail varnish cracked, wisps of red hair fell untidily round her ears from a badly pinned bun, and a cigarette hung from her lower lip.

"Who should I say it is?" Her accent was Belfast with Liverpool overtones.

"Just a couple of his mates."

"Do you have names?"

"Er, Dennis and Sydney." Then Glass made his mistake. She was about to shut the door whilst she went to fetch him when the detective put his foot in the way. That meant only one thing to the Irish woman.

"Patsy," she screamed. "It's the coppers. Patsy!" A door burst open at the back and a man ran out.

"Stay where you are," he shouted. He was brandishing a gun.

"The house is surrounded, Kelly," warned Glass. Had Tony Snow's men arrived?

"Just get out of my way." He came forward, still holding the gun. The woman was beside him. It was a narrow hall, hardly wide enough for them to pass. Glass moved to pull Moon back towards the front door. Kelly mistook his action. " I warned you," he screamed. He pulled the trigger. The bullet tore into Glass's thigh, just below the groin. He fell to the ground. Moon ran forward at Kelly, defenceless. Kelly allowed the Sergeant to reach him, then smashed the butt of the gun on the back of his unprotected head. Moon slumped unconscious over Glass's splayed legs. " Come on, we're getting out," shouted Kelly, and dragged the girl to the door. Glass valiantly tried to grab his ankle, but Kelly side-stepped him and booted him cruelly in the face. The Irish girl spat at him and she too was gone.

Glass felt a throbbing pain in his thigh and put his hand down to feel. His trousers were soaked and the warm wet blood soaked his hand. His nose bled, too, and he feared it might be broken.

He struggled to sit up and peered over the supine figure of Sergeant Moon. " Wake up, son. Are you all right?" He shook him gently. Moon groaned, and Glass sank back, relieved. His own leg still hurt. This was not going to look good at Scotland Yard.

However, by the time they heard about Glass, Scotland Yard had more to worry about.

That night, The Executioner claimed his second victim.

SIXTEEN

Robert Trevellyn lay on the hard single bed in his cell at Wormwood Scrubs. His first five days in prison had been more arduous than he had anticipated. He had been attacked in the exercise yard when a group of his fellow prisoners formed a circle round him whilst another struck him with a pick. Seven stitches were needed in his face. Then, in the dining-room, several men had stubbed out lighted cigarettes on his body. On both occasions he felt that the warders had not shown much enthusiasm in coming to his rescue. Now he was in solitary confinement " for his own safety ". He would like to have had the opportunity to deal with his malefactors one at a time. His eyes gleamed when he thought of what he would do to them.

The expression on his face at the Old Bailey had not lied. He felt no remorse for the old man he had killed, nor for his widow. Of course, he had managed to fool the probation officer, but that had been easy. In fact, he was rather proud of himself. His first killing had gone well. He had come a long way since he stoned strung-up cats to death in primary school. He had conducted the whole affair with as much efficiency as his heroes in " The Clockwork Orange ". He had seen the film nineteen times. He still did not care for Beethoven, but he enjoyed the way they beat up the old tramp and tortured the woman. His victim had pleaded with him too, begged him with tears in his eyes. And blood coming out of his mouth. And the old lady sobbing as her husband was beaten to death in front of her. Trevellyn savoured the moment. They had offered him all their money. Fifteen pounds. But it was not the money he did it for.

He heard a key turn in the cell door and a warder peered distastefully inside. " Padre to see you, Trevellyn." He showed in a man in clerical garb. He appeared younger than the average priest and his sideboards suggested grey tinting. " I'll leave it to you, Father. Ring when you want to leave."

" God bless you, my son," opened the Padre. " How are

you?"

" I didn't ask to see you."

" No, no, the pleasure is all mine," said the other pleasantly. " I believe you killed a man."

" So what?"

" I am here to be of service."

" You are no service to me, coming in here to quote the fucking Bible."

" There is only one part of the Bible I would quote to you, son. Exodus, Chapter 21, Verse 24. ' Eye for eye, tooth for tooth, hand for hand, foot for foot '." The priest's voice changed during the sentence from a pious tenor to a threatening baritone. It was noticeable enough to make the youth to look up.

In time to see a hypodermic syringe in the other's hand.

" Hey, what," were the only words he managed. The needle slid easily through the thin sleeve of Her Majesty's garment. The unlikely ecclesiastic moved quickly. He took a rope from beneath his robes, tied it round the youth's neck in a slip knot and tightened it to the point where breathing was obstructed but not terminated.

"According to the chemist, Trevellyn, you are still able to hear me. Just unable to move your limbs." Recognition fluttered in the murderer's eyes. Along with fear. " I have brought you some photographs. This is the man you killed." He waved them in front of Trevellyn's face. " I should like you to remember his cries when he died begging for mercy. You will not be able to scream of course," he added, conversationally. " This is his wife. Remember her grief at your trial? I should like you to have it on your mind as you pass over. Strangulation is a painful death. I am afraid I was not able to arrange anything as grand as a scaffold, but this rope works just as well."

Trevellyn understood every word. The trouble was, his his body would not function. He pressed muscles in response to his brain's instructions, but nothing moved. Now he experienced the physical manifestations of stark terror, the prickly perspiring pores, the nausea in the pit of the stomach, the sudden uncontrollable evacuation of the bowels and the parched throat.

Throat. His throat hurt as the rope made final inroads against his Adam's apple. His face swelled like a purple balloon, blood trapped in his head. He could not breath out or in.

For the first time he began to regret his actions, but by the time his lips could form the word " sorry ", the life-giving oxygen could not reach his lungs and only God was able to hear it.

Cooly, the " padre " dragged the body over to the bed, laid it on the mattress and removed the rope from the neck. He extracted a card from beneath his cloak and folded it under Trevellyn's lapel. Then he rang the bell.

" Father Angelucci not able to come tonight?" said the warder as he opened the cell door.

" A touch of sciatica, I believe." He pointed to the still body. " He is resting."

" A tough nut that one. They had to put him in here to protect him from the other men. They would have maimed him."

" Yes, it is as well."

" I reckon you are wasting your time there," opined the officer. He locked the door after them and walked along the corridor with The Executioner.

" Oh, I don't know. I like to think I have had some effect in bringing him closer to God. Start off his new life on the right foot so to speak."

" I don't know about that, Father. I reckon the only way to treat these hard cases is to make them knuckle under. It is the law of the jungle with them. Violence is the only language they understand. No disrespect, but you get to learn that in this job. Give them an inch and they'll trample all over you." They reached the door.

" I am sure you are right," agreed the other with a warm smile, and before he could reply he shook his hand firmly. " God be with you." And, with a wave of valediction, he departed.

SEVENTEEN

Tuesday, March 16th

It was early morning before prison officers found the body of Robert Trevellyn. At first it was thought he was ill and in a coma, then one of the warders observed the small card with the gallows on it sticking out from under his lapel and they knew.

" This means you will have to extend your list," the Assistant Commissioner told Knox. " It would now appear that none of the men in Her Majesty's Prisons are safe from The Executioner."

" How did he get in?" asked Knox. " I have only just heard the news."

" The easy way. Just drove in through the main gate."

" Just like that?"

" He was dressed as a priest. Told the man on the gate

that the usual padre was sick. He never thought twice about it. They are more concerned with people trying to break out. This was a new experience for them, someone breaking in."

"Presumably he broke out again, as it were, without any trouble."

"Even gave the security man a cigar."

Knox pondered. "I don't think I would worry about extending the list, sir. He would never try the same trick again."

"I would put nothing past this man, Robin."

"I wonder what his next move will be."

"We shall have to wait until he writes to tell us, shan't we?" replied the Assistant Commissioner acidly. "And The Executioner is not all of our problems this morning." He told Knox about the shooting of Chief Inspector Glass.

"Is he badly hurt?"

"He is in Liverpool Royal Infirmary with a bullet in his leg and Sergeant Moon is being detained under observation with concussion." He spread his hands in a gesture of helplessness like a Frenchman feeling for raindrops. "It is one thing after the other. I want you to go down to the Scrubs this morning and see if you can find anything at all there. And talk to Trevellyn's parents. They might have had some intimation of his demise, a letter or something."

"Unlikely, isn't it, sir?"

"Extremely. But, as always with this case, we are clutching at straws, Chief Inspector. Have none of our usual informers come up with anything?"

"Not a word. There is a lot of unrest amongst the criminal classes since THe Executioner started in business. The forged passport trade is booming. I reckon we will have the biggest exodus of villains since the days of transportation."

"Well, keep at it, Robin. Continue the man-to-man watches for the time being."

Knox went first to Wormwood Scrubs.

"This has shaken us," confessed the Governor, inviting Knox into his office. The inference is that if people can get in here so easily, they could get out easily as well. There is to be an enquiry about security. My head is on the block."

"What is the reaction amongst the men?"

"Most of them are frightened to death. Seven are on hunger strike in case their meals are poisoned, and three have elected to become criminally insane and have requested tranfers to Broadmoor."

"Have you found out what happened to the real priest?"

"Father Angelucci? He received a telephone call purporting to be from the prison, telling him to cancel his evening visit because of some trouble in the cells."

"And nobody had a description of the imposter?"

"All anybody really noticed was his clerical collar. His face was in the shadows. But you will find that people very rarely notice features behind a uniform."

Trevellyn's parents arrived at noon. His father was a short man with a pointed head and long straggly hair which looked ridiculous at forty and would have earned him a place in the Afghan Hound class at Crufts. His manner was servile, and the obvious boss of the family was Mrs. Trevellyn who's muscular body suggested a member of the English discus throwing team.

"Somebody will pay for this," she declared. "I'll see to that. They can't get away with it." She turned to her husband. "Say something, Father." Mr. Trevellyn opened his mouth, thought better of it and shut it again. "Oh, he's hopeless. No good talking to him. Where have you put my little boy?"

"We will take you to him in a minute," said the Governor. "But first, Detective Chief Inspector Knox here would like to ask you a few questions."

"Oh, would he? Well, I'd like to ask him a few questions. Like how can my son get killed in a place like this, and I know the answer, too. The police killed him, that's what. I know what goes on. Just because I only work in a factory I'm not supposed to know, but I do, let me tell you. They can't fool me." Knox vainly tried to intervene, but she continued her tirade. "What have you got to say, copper? Got your defence ready, have you?"

"I just wanted to ask if you have received any intimation of your son's death; any letters or threatening phone calls."

"I wouldn't need to, would I? We all know who done it, don't we?" Without warning she pushed Knox in the stomach. "I want to see my son."

The Governor coughed delicately. "I will take you down, Mrs. Trevellyn. He shrugged his shoulders at Knox. The Chief Inspector nodded and took his leave and returned to Scotland Yard.

"No joy, sir?" asked Sergeant Evans who was midway through his apricot sponge in the canteen.

"None at all. Strangled like Debbings. No rope this time, he took it away."

"Probably holding his cassock up."

"The same card with the gallows and not a fingerprint in sight."

"Back to the records then?"

"I suppose so. We'll keep the plan going for the time being."

After his lunch he phoned Sue.

"You didn't ring last night," she accused.

" I'm sorry. I didn't get the chance. Did you see the papers on Sunday?"

" The letter, you mean? Yes. We were in Newby Bridge when I read it and I thought of you." She could have added that she thought of him for most of the weekend.

" Well, that is why I have been busy."

" Do you really think he will kill someone?"

" He already did. Last night. It is in tonight's papers."

" He doesn't waste much time. So you are tied up again then?"

" I could manage dinner."

" Really?" The pleasure sounded in her voice.

" I'll pick you up at eight."

He took her to an Italian restaurant in Chelsea. She treated herself to a bottle of Rive Gauche in Selfridges and wore it liberally. They ate lasagne.

" Did you have a good weekend," he forced himself to ask.

" We went to Carlisle to interview the people at the Post Office robbery."

" Did you see Chief Inspector Glass?"

" No. We missed him by ten minutes. Tim saw him on Sunday, but I was still in bed. I'll see him tomorrow though. You knew he had been injured? Well, Tim is bringing him home from Liverpool and I'm going along for the ride. It's my day off."

" You are becoming quite involved with Scotland Yard one way and another."

She laughed. " I suppose I am. I'd say your case was more fun than the Post Office robberies. The Eexecutioner. Sounds very romantic, like an Edgar Wallace story."

" Someone else said that, and it is not romantic at all. He is a murderer, too."

"Oh, but not in the same way. He stands for justice."
It was strange how she had stuck up for him a few days
earlier, she thought, and probably would again. But she
didn't agree with him at all.

"You have been listening to your reporter friend. Does
Chief Inspector Glass think that way too?"

"Of course, doesn't everybody?" Her eyes opened in
mock innocence. "Listen Robin. Last week a policeman's
son was killed and the murderer was given twelve months.
Twelve months! If someone killed me would you be satis-
fied that justice had been done if you met the killer walking
down the street nine months later? The law is an ass."

"Better an ass than no law at all." But he conjectured
her question. "I would want to kill him," he said at last,
"but the whole point of civilisation is that we overcome
and control such base feelings."

"All right, if not for revenge, how about prevention?
Nine months in jail is not too much a deterrent in anyone's
eyes."

"Sue, Sue." Knox put down his knife and took her hand
in his. "I want us to enjoy ourselves when we go out, not
fight. Let's have some champagne instead.

It was a good night. They went on to Tramps and ended
up at Robin's flat where Sue cuddled close to him in his
five-foot bed. Luxury!

Detective Chief Inspector Glass slept on an iron three-
foot rack.

EIGHTEEN

For reasons of space, Detective Chief Inspector Glass occupied a bed in the men's public ward at Liverpool Royal Infirmary.

His injury was not serious. The bullet had been removed and was on exhibition in a jar on his bedside table for all who cared to see. He still had, in his flat, a similar jar containing his pickled appendix which was removed in 1936. He thought the two jars would make an interesting pair of matching bookends.

His leg, though painful, was healing satisfactorily, and the only treatment he had to undergo was rest. His pride was causing him the most discomfort. Patsy Kelly and his lady friend (" moll " as Glass was inclined to call her) had escaped the diligent watchers of Superintendent Snow by posing as a courting couple and canoodling their way past the police car guarding the house, to disappear into the night.

Sergeant Moon lay in the next bed, pale and inert. He had been recumbent thus for most of the day. Glass had tried once or twice to talk to him but without much response other than the odd guttural croak.

" He will be as right as rain in the morning," a nurse assured him. " When that nasty headache has gone." The nasty headache had been caused less by the previous night's blow than by the adverse ministrations of a student nurse. A Rhodesian. Full of good meaning, she had put the radio headphones round his ears in the hope that a little light music might cheer him up. Unhappily, the wires had become entangled, the headphones had jammed on his head and Moon had been forced to listen to Radio One at full volume for two hours until rescued by a porter with pliers.

Because of his companion's torpescence, Glass had been forced to seek social intercourse with his neighbour on the opposite side, a Stoneycroft crane operator who was suffering from some obscure trouble with his ileum complicated by cicatricial stenosis of the bowel.

" It's me guts," he explained to Glass. " They've had to send for more rubber sheets, you know. I've got through the lot in this place."

" Really," said the Chief Inspector, who was enjoying his apple crumble at the time.

" Yes indeed. They say I'm the worst case they've had in here for rubber sheets."

Glass put down his dish and averted his eyes from the other's bed. He was glad he only had to stop just the one day in hospital. He had read all the newspapers that had been brought into the ward, and he had drunk the half bottle of Lucozade sent across by a sympathetic benefactor with gallstones.

In the evening, he had to suffer visiting hour. A morose collection of mixed relatives assembled in moribund groups beside each bed and ate steadily through several pounds of soft fruit. He was relieved that none of them stopped by to talk to him. All the time he kept his eyes on the door for Salvation Army visitors who might force themselves upon him against his will and try to rally him and make him buy copies of *War Cry*.

On the other hand, he was not looking forward greatly

133

to going home. There would be repercussions at Scotland Yard when they got round to discussing his ineptitude in the case. Permitting the only suspect to casually walk to freedom in the throes of embrace would not help his standing at the Yard. There would be the usual accusations that he was trying to run the show alone.

By Wednesday, however, Scotland Yard were not only involved in Trevellyn's murder, they had another surprise waiting. The third letter from The Executioner arrived at the offices of *The Times*.

NINETEEN

Wednesday, March 17th

The Times printed the third letter from The Executioner

Dear Sir,

I have now demonstrated that nobody is beyond my reach. The Arm of The Executioner is longer than the Arm of the law.

For my next victim, it will stretch even further, to a murderer whom the law has been unable even to trace.

The law should have punished Robert Trevellyn, but his sentence was a mockery to the name of justice.

My sentences will not be so.

Watch for the sign of the gallows.

THE EXECUTIONER

By now, The Executioneer had become a public hero. *The Megaphone*, in the person of Timothy Slade, described him as a Twentieth Century Robin Hood, and the Editor of the paper, in the leader column, hoped that the affair would cause judges and magistrates alike to toughen their sentences for violent offenders.

"The reduction of a crime from murder to manslaughter," he wrote, "devalues the currency of human life. The result is the increasing violence we see in our society today."

All the other papers carried articles in a similar vein, and the great majority of letters supported the campaign of The Executioner. Private citizens were mounting their own, more law-abiding, efforts, and the demand for action became so great that the Home Secretary was forced to announce the setting-up of a Government Enquiry into the whole question of Crime and Punishment.

Meanwhile, Detective Chief Inspector Knox was still endeavouring to trace The Executioner.

"So much for my list now," he told Sergeant Evans. "We might as well call the whole operation off."

"He could be bluffing."

"He never has before."

"True." Evans looked again at the letter. "What do you reckon this means? Somebody we don't even know has committed a crime?"

"I don't read it like that," said Knox. "I think he is after some villain that we are already chasing. What have we got on the unsolved list at the moment? There are these Post Office jobs for a start. We don't know which firm is doing those."

"Handy for us if he caught them, really."

"You are joking, Sergeant Evans. Think of the headlines

' Executioner Succeeds Where Yard Fail '."

" Ah yes. I see what you mean, sir. How is Glass getting on, by the way? Is he still in hospital?"

" Coming out today. Sue is picking him up as a matter of fact."

" *Your* Sue?"

" *My* Sue. She is going up with Slade. He is a friend of Glass."

" Slade the reporter? Wasn't it him that she spent the weekend with in the Lake District?" muttered Sergeant Evans pedantically.

" Yes," snapped Knox.

" This is the same Sue, isn't it, for whom you were proclaiming your undying love and devotion a few days ago?"

" You know perfectly well it is."

" Ah." Evans playfully whistled the opening bars of " True Love " from " High Society ", a tuneless rendition that would have caused no problem for Ronnie Ronalde.

" He is no good for her. Him and his Robin Hood notions. Do you know she is beginning to take The Executioner's side. Says she hopes that if we catch him we will let him go for performing a public service. And Glass thinks that The Executioner is the finest figure of British justice since Pierrepoint."

" I used to know Albert Pierrepoint," mused Sergeant Evans. " A grand chap. He ran a pub near Preston called the Rose and Crown. Have you read his book, sir? It is well worth looking at."

" All I can say is, it is a good job Glass is not on this case. He'd end up awarding him the George Cross. I tell you, Evans, I'll nail this fellow. I only need half a chance and I'll nail him."

TWENTY

Detective Chief Inspector Glass was waiting forlornly in his bed when Sue and Timothy Slade arrived to collect him from the hospital. He wore a long woollen garment which had started life as a blue dressing-gown, and he was replete with fried haddock and chips.

"Thank God you have arrived," he said. "Another five minutes and I would have had to eat the suet pudding."

"This is Sue Owen," introduced Timothy.

Glass took her hand. "They've taken away my trousers, you know, so I could not have left without you."

"Where is your sergeant?"

Glass pointed to the bed alongside. "I think he is sleeping again. He has slept a lot since the accident."

"You never told me about this Liverpool lead."

"Came up at the last minute," lied Glass. "But the scoop would have been yours. If I hadn't let him get away," he added glumly.

"No news on his recapture?"

"We haven't captured him once yet, but no, not a word. He has gone to ground somewhere. I will find him though," stated the Chief Inspector defiantly, tugging on the cord of his dressing-gown to emphasise his point.

The Sister arrived and set in motion the procedure for the detectives' release. Sergeant Moon was woken and given a form listing several unpleasant symptoms that he might experience in the course of the next forty-eight hours.

If any did occur, he was to report to his nearest casualty centre.

"We shall be home in three hours," assured Timothy Slade as he led them out to the Audi.

On the journey they discussed The Executioner. "He has worked quickly," said Glass approvingly. "It is only six days since we were both at the Old Bailey at Trevellyn's trial."

"Robin Knox says he will catch him," said Sue.

"How on earth do you know him?" asked Glass.

"She knows everybody," said Timothy Slade.

"I think he could wait a bit," said Glass. "Give The Executioner a few more months and he will have cleaned up crime in this country and we can all have a bit of a rest."

They reached Sergeant Moon's house in three hours, seventeen minutes. Ethel was waiting for him on the doorstep, and behind her stood a stout formidable woman with folded arms and bloodless thin lips.

"Ethel's mother," explained Moon as he gathered his case. The others nodded sympathetically.

"Take the rest of the day off, Sergeant," said Glass magnanimously, eyeing the gorgon with some misgiving. They left Moon to his fate and continued to the Chief Insector's flat.

"My car is still at the Yard," said Glass.

"Do you want dropping there then?"

"Good Lord, no. I'd be up before the Assistant Commissioner and given two hours to find the killers. Anyway, it will rust more slowly in their garage."

Mrs. Cowan, the landlady, watched his arrival from her vantage point behind the sitting-room net curtains and was in the hall to intercept them. "Your rent is due on Saturdays, Mr. Glass. Today is Wednesday."

" I've been away, Mrs. Cowan." He limped theatrically and extended his bad leg as evidence to support his excuse for absence.

" Well, I wish you would let me know about these things. I didn't know whether to let your room or what."

" Yes, I've only been here eleven years. I can see the reason for your doubt."

" I didn't know what had happened to you. Worried for your safety I was."

" Then you should have rung for the police," snapped the Chief Inspector, and he hopped angrily up the stairs.

He made his guests a pot of Choicest tea and they discussed the Post Office robberies. " There is a hunt on for Kelly," said Glass. " He can't hide forever. Somebody will snout on him."

" I can't forget that little girl," said Timothy. " Gail Hutchinson."

" Or the policeman's wife," said Glass. " The widow's pension isn't all that much."

Sue took a digestive biscuit from the tin barrel. " What will he get when they catch him?"

" When *I* catch him, you mean? Oh, about seven years would you say, Tim?"

" But that is ridiculous," said Sue.

" Precisely. What we have been saying all along. And don't forget, there may be more to come."

There was.

Nothing happened for the next two days then on the morning of Saturday, March 20, Easter Saturday, the Post Office gang struck again.

TWENTY-ONE

Easter Saturday, March 20th

Mrs. Catherine Taylor-Brocklehurst, at the age of seventy-three, lived in a penthouse apartment in Lytham St. Annes. Her husband had built up a textile business between the wars and, by the time of his death from a coronary due to overwork, had amassed enough money to enable her to eke out her retirement in idle luxury.

She shared the apartment with two chihuahuas, Matthew and Jane, and a cockatoo, Simba, a savage bird that had drawn blood on two occasions and was prevented only by a stout chain attached to her scaly ankle from pecking the miniscule dogs to death.

Mrs. Taylor-Brocklehurst took the *Daily Telegraph*, ground her own coffee, drank malt whisky aged in wood, and spent most of her evenings playing bridge with ladies of similar ilk.

The Government extracted penal taxes from her investment income, but such was the magnitude of her late husband's fortune that she did not anticipate declining into abject poverty before 1998 by which time she could well expect to be dead.

It was her custom on a Saturday morning to visit her hairdresser (Mr. Derrick of St. Anne's, who wore men's cosmetics and moonlighted in the evenings as a drag artiste in Manchester working men's clubs). She favoured gentle waves and a blue tint to match her veins. After a stroll round the shops and a coffee and Danish pasty in the Square, she would walk slowly home for her lunch, calling at the local office to collect her pension.

On Easter Saturday, she became the most important person in Britain—the first eye witness to give a description of one of the post office robbers.

She did not realise it at the time. She was a good hundred yards from the post office when the two men ran out to the waiting car. She advanced fifty yards whilst they tried to start the vehicle and came abreast of the bonnet when they eventually fired the engine. Mere curiosity prompted her to look into the car, where upon she was startled to see a man in a mask looking back at her. This made her peer closer. She observed a man in the passenger seat, not wearing a mask, who reminded her of her nephew Lionel, a forty-year-old physiotherapist who made a living massaging white women in Johannesburg.

The car drove off and she turned into the post office where further surprises awaited her. Mr. Emmanual Twigg, the white-haired postmaster and stalwart of the local church choir, lay across the counter in a pool of blood.

Mrs. Taylor-Brocklehurst was not a lady of faint heart. Blood did not frighten her. She walked calmly round the counter, lifted Mr. Twigg's head and inspected it for the source of flow, which transpired to be just above the left temple. She took a clean handkerchief from her handbag and pressed it firmly on the wound which had already started to clot. She felt for his pulse and was relieved to find that his heart was beating normally. Only then did she calmly pick up the nearby telephone and dial 999 for the police.

An hour later, the St. Annes sub-post office had been turned into an incident room under the command of Detective Inspector Moorcroft.

"All under control," he told Glass on the telephone to Scotland Yard. "No need for you to come up."

"Was there much taken?" asked Glass wearily. His leg was playing him up, and the paperwork that had accumulated on his desk during his absence tended to make it ache more.

"Two thousand pounds in all. But the shopkeeper is O.K. Bit of a bump on the head. Butt of a gun I shouldn't wonder." Glass thought of Sergeant Moon. "Better than shooting him though."

"You haven't managed to trace the car then?"

"Fraid not. Mrs. Taylor-Brocklehurst is good on faces but bad on cars."

"Mrs. Who?"

"The witness. How's the leg by the way?"

"I'm considering amputation," said Glass. "Tell me about this witness."

"Pretty clear picture. Chap in his twenties. We are having the Identikit picture sent across to you, to check in the files."

"Does he remind you of Patsy Kelly by any chance?"

Moorcroft thought. "Bit of a likeness I suppose. Same eyes. Different colour hair though and different shaped head. No, not really like him. No news on Kelly yet?"

"We have circulated his picture, but he has obviously been hiding out somewhere. Looks as though he is about again now though, in his old haunts, too."

"You still think he is the one?"

"I would lay even money on it now. Did you ever find out if he had a brother?"

" Definitely no brother. He came from a broken home though."

" Don't they all?"

" What I mean is, the mother married again. She might have had children."

" Step-brothers you mean? Of course." Glass thumped the desk, annoyed that he had not thought of that. He lit a Craven A.

" I believe they live in Liverpool," said Moorcroft.

" Dingle to be exact," said Glass, pleased to get in his bit of knowledge.

" You've been to see her? Does Patsy live with her?"

" No, he is shacked up with some Irish tart."

" Well, anything I can do this end, let me know."

" I will," promised Glass. " Happy Easter."

" Shouldn't we be in St. Annes ourselves?" asked Sergeant Moon, who was standing beside the Chief Inspector.

" No point. We will have the picture on the teleprinter any minute and then we can start looking."

" We have been looking for three days already."

" For Kelly, yes. This is the other man. They can't hide out forever. Every newspaper in Britain will carry their pictures tomorrow. The whole country will be looking out for them."

" But you don't have any faith in the public. You have always said they are a waste of time."

" Quite right, too."

" So . . ." But Glass cut him short.

" Look, Sergeant Moon, stop arguing. I have got this case nearly solved. We have just received the most important information we have had so far." He paused for a moment to allow this to sink in. " Patsy Kelly's mother married again," he announced dramatically, " and may have more children."

Moon's face remained blank. "I don't see . . ."

"These children will be Patsy's step-brothers. Remember, he is supposed to knock around with his brother? Well, they will have DIFFERENT NAMES."

"Which means . . ."

"Which means, Sergeant, that we might well have a name to put to that face. No wonder we didn't find any Kellys in Hill Street. Get me Superintendent Snow at Liverpool on the phone."

Moon did as he was bid. The process took ten minutes but, finally, the Merseyside officer came on the line.

"Tony? Walter Glass here. You know Patsy Kelly's mother in Hill Street? You don't happen to know her name since she remarried, do you? Or if she has any kids by this husband?"

"Not a clue, but I can find out for you, Walter, no problem. I'll ring you back later. How's the leg?"

"Pretty grim," said Glass, who was prone to hypochondria. "I'm keeping my eyes open for gangrene."

"What do we do now?" asked Moon when Glass had replaced the phone.

"I am going home," stated the Chief Inspector. "To rest my leg you understand. When the picture comes through, send copies to the agencies and press. Then you can wait for Superintendent Snow to ring, and on your way home drop by at my place and tell me what he says."

Moon did not like to mention that Notting Hill Gate was not on the way to Golder's Green.

Glass drove home in his A35, attaining a speed of forty m.p.h. with a downwind on the Bayswater Road. He wanted to be in by five to check his pools coupon. Every week he dreamed of winning a two hundred and twenty thousand pounds fortune on the Treble Chance to enable him to leave the Force and start a mink farm in Sussex, but the nearest he came was in 1948 when his second dividend in June of that year paid for two seats at the cinema with a vanilla ice cream at the interval.

He made it with time to spare, and by 5 p.m. when the football results came on Radio Two, he was firmly ensconced on his settee, a cup of tea and a packet of biscuits by his side and a folded copy of *The Megaphone* in his hand on which to take down the scores.

"Blackburn Rovers 0, Burnley 3. Blackpool 1, Millwall 1. Cardiff . . ." The front doorbell rang. Glass cursed, put down his paper and hopped over to the door. It was Sue Owen.

"What a surprise," he said warmly. "Come on in and shut up a minute while I take down the scores."

"Charming!" She smiled and followed him in.

"I've just brewed up. You'll find the pot in the kitchen over there." He returned to his marking while she poured herself a drink.

"How is the leg?" she asked when the Scottish League Division Two had been tabulated.

"Terrible. I'm thinking of getting a new one. I might write to Douglas Bader and find out where he gets his. Chocolate biscuit?" He handed across the packet. "McVitie & Price's Plain Chocolate Wholemeal. I could live on these."

"Not very sustaining. Do you have normal food as well?"

"When I have time in between cases."

"How is the post office thing going?"

"There was another robbery this morning in St. Annes. This time we have a description of the other man." Glass

145

poured himself a second cup of tea from the pot she had brought in. " Anyway, to what do I owe the pleasure of this call?"

" Just curious to see where you lived. And to see how your leg was, of course. Heard anything from Tim?"

" Ah," said Glass. " So that is the reason."

" Not at all. I just wondered how he was. I haven't seen him since the day we went to Liverpool to bring you home."

" Big romance between you two, is it?"

" No. We just go out and have a good time."

" ' Just good friends ' they used to call it in my day. In inverted commas."

" I know all about your day, thank you very much."

" He's not a bad lad, Tim," said Glass.

" He's fun to go out with." Sue brushed the crumbs from the thighs of her ski-tight denims. " Tell me what you know about Robin Knox?"

" Oh yes, you never did say how you knew him."

" I asked first."

" A very clever policeman. All college and blackboards of course as it all is nowadays, but he has done better than most."

" Mmmm, I wonder what he has got to hate," said Sue pensively.

" I don't follow you," said Glass. " Hate?"

" I have a theory that hate is the best spur to success that there is. You will always find that the people that get on in the world often come from broken homes or have unhappy schooldays or some physical disability. Achieving success is their way of turning round to the world and saying ' I made it, so sod you!' "

" Quite the psychologist."

" It works. Take Timothy for instance. The perfect example."

" What chip on his shoulder has he got?"

" The classic. Illegitimate son of a nobleman. Brought up in comparative poverty with no claim to the title. Determined to make it on his own and show the bastards, as it were, that he is as good as them."

" I never knew that about Slade," said Glass curiously. " His father disowned him, did he?"

" No. Oddly enough, they were on quite good terms. I think Tim's father still kept in touch with his mother on the quiet, she never married, and he and Tim were pretty close. I know Tim was most upset when he died."

" How long ago was that?"

" I don't know. A couple of years I think. I didn't know him then and he doesn't usually talk about it."

" You don't know his father's name?"

" Good Lord, no. The old Duchess, or whatever she was, obviously thought she was better off staying put, so the whole thing was hushed up. She would go berserk if it ever got out."

" But isn't there the chance Tim might try to claim on the estate?"

" That's the last thing he would do. He has made it all on his own and he has never told anyone who his father is, and very few people know what I have just told you. Which I should not really have done."

" It is my job, allowing people to tell me things they shouldn't. That is how I have made my reputation as a brilliant detective."

" Keeping your mouth shut must be another of your attributes. You have still not told me anything about Robin."

"Robin, eh?"

"We met at a club if you must know. He has taken me out a couple of times and he is very nice."

"But you don't know what it is he hates?"

"Now you are teasing me."

"Did you ever hear how Timothy Slade's father died?"

"No, I don't think so. From the way he talks, I would say unexpectedly. A heart attack, maybe."

"Mmmmm." Glass appeared lost in thought.

"You were telling me about Detective Chief Inspector Knox," persisted Sue, but Glass was saved from answering by another ring of the doorbell.

"It is like Victoria Station up here sometimes," he grumbled.

"I'll go. You rest your leg."

The visitor was Sergeant Moon, bearing tidings from Superintendent Snow in Liverpool.

"Lots of information, sir. Mrs. Kelly's new name is Mrs. O'Malley. She has eight children by this husband. The first was a boy, Brendan, and the other seven were girls."

"How old is the boy now?"

"About twenty. But he doesn't live with his mother. He left home at eleven, farmed out to relatives somewhere up North."

"Greenland, you mean?"

"More like Preston I believe, sir. Anyway, he left there at fifteen and nobody seems to know where he is now."

"I've got a good idea where he was this morning. In St. Annes with his step-brother." Glass rolled his eyes skywards like a white Al Jolson. "O'Malley, O'Malley. The name rings a bell, and I am sure I have seen his picture before. Have you got it with you, Moon?"

The Sergeant produced the dotted likeness, and Glass

studied it earnestly.

Sue spoke to Moon. " Would you like a cup of tea?"

" I wouldn't say no," said Moon, mindful of the long journey ahead to Golder's Green.

" I'll have another cup myself," said Glass, without getting up. Sue took his cup and went into the kitchen. The Chief Inspector took his pools coupon out of his inside pocket and started to check his predictions against the results. Moon embarked on a vigorous consumption of the chocolate biscuits.

" Any joy?" asked Sue, coming in with the tea.

" Twenty points in one line," said Glass. " But it isn't enough. There are thirteen score draws." He studied the results again. " Who would have thought that Millwall would have drawn at Blackpool?"

" Perhaps the sea air did them good," said Sue. " I am afraid I know nothing about football." Moon knew even less and wisely concentrated on the chocolate biscuits. But Glass was staring ahead with a fanatical gleam in his eye.

" Get me *The Megaphone*," he shouted at the startled Moon.

" It is in your hand," pointed out Sue. " You wrote the results on it."

" So I did." He unravelled the paper and feverishly turned the pages.

Sue looked at Moon, her eyebrows asking the question.

" I don't know," replied the Sergeant. " But he will no doubt tell me before the end of the week."

" I will tell you on Monday, Sergeant Moon. I am going to take you for a day out in London."

" Anywhere in particular, sir?"

" Beside the river."

" Why Monday?" asked Sue. " Why can't you take him

out tomorrow?"

"Because tomorrow," said Glass grandly, "I am going to help your friend Robin Knox catch The Executioner."

TWENTY-TWO

Easter Day, March 21st

The Mansion known as Grange Manor had been the home of the Highly family since 1759. One Basil Highly had acquired the land by a combination of rape, pillage and gambling. Once he had installed himself as local Squire, he turned respectable and controlled the affairs of the village with a kind smile, a gentle word and a sharp aim with the duelling pistol.

Future generations of the family conveniently forgot their bloody ancestry and became respected members of the community, collecting more acres and a title along the way. The reversal in fortune began after the First World War when the first echoes of Socialism were heard and the crippling death duties reduced the estate to a large garden. However, the title still remained and the last Lord Highly (Neville Harold Sydney—the 12th Lord) had managed to survive on his appearance money at the House of Lords.

Upon the demise of His Lordship, the old house took on an air of faded gentility. Only a small household staff (butler, cook and housekeeper) was retained to look after the needs of Lady Highly in her widowhood. She and the late Lord had no children and her only companion was a

Siamese cat called Badger.

The rich cream anaglypta walls of yesterday were now a sandy beige, and pieces of stucco had crumbled from the outside of the building. The scullery, pantry and kitchen were untouched by modernisation, but the house still kept its character with its wide staircase, carved balustrade and moulded ceilings, plus, of course, the antiques and heirlooms that were relics of more prosperous days.

Glass drove his A35 up the winding driveway and parked by the stone pillars that framed the oak front door.

"This is how we guardians of the public ought to be living," he said to Sergeant Moon whom he had brought along for the ride. "This place will end up as a Social Security Gift Centre where lucky recipients will come to collect their prizes for staying off work the longest." He got out of the car. "You stay here, I shan't be more than an hour." He went over and pressed the bell set in the stone wall. The chimes of Notre Dame Cathedral echoed within.

The butler opened the door. Glass addressed him with an air of authority.

"Detective Chief Inspector Glass. Is Lady Highly at home?"

"If you would step into the hall, sir, I will ascertain if Her Ladyship is available."

Glass stationed himself beside the oak-panelled wall, beneath the head of a giant moose, stooping slightly to avoid the possibility of being garotted by the spreading antlers in the event of sudden movement.

The butler returned. "If you would care to follow me, sir." He conducted the Chief Inspector into a huge, elegant lounge. Her Ladyship sat on a striped chaise longue beside the leaded light French windows overlooking the garden, her silver hair haloed by the afternoon sun.

" Detective Chief Inspector Glass, madam."

Glass walked forward, hand extended, his feet sinking into the deep pile of the Axminster. " Don't get up, Lady Highly."

" I was not going to, Chief Inspector. Ackers, tea for two, please."

" Yes, madam." The butler crept obsequiously away, watched with approbation by Glass who would have liked a similar domestic arrangement in his own flat. A butler would minimise his dependence on electrical gadgets like his non-automatic toaster.

" To what do I owe the pleasure of this visit," said Lady Highly. " It is three years since my husband was killed. I think you were plain Detective Inspector then."

" Have you not heard the news about his murderer?"

" I no longer subscribe to newspapers, Chief Inspector. Being in no position to influence events, I have little inclination to read about them."

" Alfred George Debbings, the man who killed Lord Highly, was found hanging from a tree in St. James's Park."

" A fitting end," approved Lady Highly. " I could not have arranged a better one myself." She stopped. " You don't think I had anything to do with it?"

" Of course not. Besides, there have been other killings. No, I wanted to talk to you about the past." He sat down at the opposite end of the chaise longue and took out his packet of Craven A. " Cigarette?" Her Ladyship took one and held it to her lips for him to light. He said, " It must be lonely for you since Lord Highly died."

She puffed on the cigarette. " I suppose it is." Her voice quivered and granules of caked face powder trembled on the ridges of wrinkled skin on her neck.

Glass leaned forward confidentially. " Lady Highly. I

know about the boy."

"Oh." Colour drained from her rouged cheeks. "How? When?"

"Quite by chance. Nobody else knows and nor do they need to."

"I never saw him, you know. His mother was one of my maids. Neville was at that age when men feel a need to prove themselves. She was sent home immediately to her family, but Neville did not shirk his obligations." The family pride was still strong. "He made sure she had enough money."

"Did he continue to see her?"

"Certainly not. He never saw either of them again. As I said, he made sure the child was provided for."

So Lord Highly had not told his wife that he had kept in touch with his illegitimate son. And Glass did not intend to disillusion her now.

"He will be about twenty now, the boy?"

"I suppose he will. More."

"What was the maid's name, Lady Highly?"

"Why should you want to know that?"

"Can I just say that I should like to know and leave it at that now?" She looked uncertain. "It has nothing to do with Lord Highly, I can promise you that."

"Her name was Sladovok," she said at last. "Petra Sladovok."

"Are you sure?"

"Quite. I hired the gel. She was Polish."

"You don't know what she called the baby?"

"Is this important to you, Chief Inspector Glass? I do not like to be reminded of the fact that it took another woman to give my husband a child."

"I did not know. I am sorry."

The butler returned with the tea on a silver tray. Lady Highly set out the cups and saucers, Royal Albert China.

"I hope you like Darjeeling," she said.

"The finest of the Indian teas," replied Glass knowledgeably. There was not much anyone could tell him about tea. "Grown over five thousand feet above sea level. Makes excellent lemon tea."

"Due to the muscatel flavour," she said, "but today you will have to make do with milk. Do you take sugar?" Glass declined. "I would help you, Chief Inspector, but I am afraid I never knew what the child was christened. Once the girl had been dismissed I washed my hands of the whole sorry occurrence."

"What happened to the maid in the end?"

"I have no idea. I told you, I had no contact with them. Neither did my husband."

"How did he pay the money?"

"By banker's order, I believe. He opened an account in the boy's name and a small amount was paid into it every month. We were not over-rich."

"And after Lord Highly's death?"

"The payments had stopped long before then, when the child was sixteen."

"Nothing for him in the will?"

"As his existence was not officially recognised, it was hardly likely."

A banker's order was hardly *un*official, but Glass let the point pass.

"Why all the sudden interest after all these years?"

"I want to find the boy. Not for who he is but for what he might have become. You are positive you do not know his name? Lives may depend on it."

"Once she left the house the matter was never mentioned again."

"Ah well, you have been most helpful. I am sorry to have distressed you by raking up the past."

Lady Highly rang the bell to summon the butler. "I trust none of our conversation will go further, Chief Inspector?"

"You have my word."

"Thank you. Ackers, the Inspector is leaving." Glass allowed himself to be shown to the door.

Moon was in the car struggling with the *Sunday Times* crossword.

"Did you get what you wanted, sir?"

"No," said Glass. "But I still think I am on the right track. Are Somerset House open on a Sunday?" Moon shook his head. "We'll try the offices of *The Megaphone*. Somebody will be there who might help us."

"What exactly are we looking for?"

"A man called Sladovok, but that is not his name."

"Oh." Moon went back to his crossword. It seemed easier.

"I'll drop you off at home if you like. I can go there on my own. I will pick you up after lunch tomorrow."

"For our day out by the river?"

"Do you like football, Sergeant Moon?"

"I have never watched it, sir."

"Then tomorrow will be a new experience for you. We are going to watch Fulham play at Craven Cottage."

"Oh." Life, thought Moon, was full of surprises.

There was a surprise the next morning for Glass.

Another post office robbery.

In Fulham.

TWENTY-THREE

Easter Monday, March 22nd

It was the most successful robbery yet.

It took place at eleven o'clock in the morning. The two masked men walked into the shop, one put the catch on the door whilst the other went up to the counter and demanded the money. There were no customers. The Fulham postmaster, Mr. Eshilby, did not argue. He had read gory reports of the wounds of previous heroes and was only too anxious to give the gunmen anything they wanted.

" I've got more postal orders in the safe," he whimpered as the man in the Yogi Bear mask denuded his till of paper currency.

" You won't send for the police for ten minutes, will you?" threatened the man in the Barney Flintstone mask. " Or should we put him to sleep to be on the safe side?" he enquired of his companion.

" No, I won't, I promise," yelped Mr. Eshilby. " Look, I'll tell you what I'll do, I'll cut the telephone wires, look." He picked up a pair of scissors and, with the dexterity of a midwife, dramatically cut the cord.

" They are improving," said Glass when they eventually arrived on the scene. " Three thousand pounds, not a witness in sight and a clean getaway."

" Practice makes perfect I suppose," sighed Moon. " But shouldn't he be closed on Easter Monday?"

"The Post Office part was. Apparently, the poor bleeder had over-ordered on Easter eggs and he had opened up this morning in a last desperate attempt to get rid of them."

"What a coincidence it should be in Fulham when we were coming here this afternoon."

"If you think that is a coincidence, Sergeant," said Glass nastily, "you ought to be ringing Walls up to see if they have any vacancies in the Sausage Department. No. I knew they would be in Fulham today. I just did not anticipate a robbery in the morning."

"If you knew they would be in Fulham, why were we not here to catch them?"

"I was not expecting them till afternoon, and don't worry, it is only one o'clock now, so we will have time for a spot of lunch before the arrest." He ushered the protesting sergeant out of the door, leaving the post office in the charge of the local uniformed officer, a black inspector who rejoiced in the name of Lance Dove.

"You'll find nothing," Glass told him helpfully. "Just make a note of what is missing and take a statement from Mr. Eshilby there. We are off to the match."

They left the officer to ponder on the congenial life in the Flying Squad and made for the nearest pub. A board on the pavement outside boasted "bar snacks" within. The choice was not large. Moon opted for a curling cheese sandwich garnished with an onion ring and a leaf of dry lettuce. Glass had an individual steak and kidney pie, reheated, with no gravy. They took these, with their beer, to a corner table in the lounge bar.

"Do you think that you can tell me what all this is about now?" begged Moon, hopefully.

Glass opened up his pie and covered the steaming interior with tomato ketchup in an attempt to camouflage the flavour.

"It is very simple," he said, "once you have worked out the connection between the places where the robberies have have taken place."

"I have not been able to work it out," admitted Moon sadly.

"Well, there is one. Each of the towns where there has been a robbery has a team in the second division of the Football League."

"But so do a lot of other towns."

"Let me finish. On the day of the first robbery at Leyton Orient, the local team were at home to Blackpool, a mid-week evening game. On the Saturday following, the day of the second robbery at Carlisle, Carlisle United were at home," he paused for emphasis, "again to Blackpool. The third robbery was at St. Annes which is down the road from Blackpool, and on that day Blackpool themselves were the home team."

"And today, I take it, Blackpool are playing at Fulham."

"You've got it, lad. It was Sue who first gave me the idea when I was checking my coupon. I mentioned something about Millwall doing well to draw at Blackpool and she said it must have been the sea air. That made me think of our trip up there, and it struck me how everything in this case kept coming back to Blackpool. The getaway car from the first robbery turned up there, Patsy Kelly originated there, then came the third robbery in St. Annes. And then, Sergeant Moon, I remembered where I had heard the name of O'Malley. I checked the Identikit picture with the football paper and I was right."

"Yes?"

"Brendan O'Malley is the Blackpool centre forward who scored the equaliser against Millwall last Saturday."

" And will he be in the team this afternoon ?"

" He will. And that is when I shall arrest him."

" Have you alerted the local police ?"

" No. I don't want to scare him off. I shall do this my way."

" But you did Patsy Kelly your way," pointed out Moon unkindly. " Where does he fit in, by the way ?"

" Knowing his record, I would imagine it was all his idea. He realised what a good cover-up the football team would be. For a start, O'Malley would have the team coach as perfect cover for getting the money out of the town without chance of being stopped. If Kelly had been stopped in the Ford Executive, he might have been done for driving a stolen car, but there would have been nothing in there to connect him with the robbery."

" Ingenous. But where will Kelly be now ? On his way back up North ?"

" I am relying on O'Malley to tell us that."

" Do you think he will ?"

" He will when I have finished with him." Glass pushed away his plate and downed a pint of Newcastle Brown in thirteen seconds. " Right, let's go."

" One thing," said Moon.

" What's that ?"

" Yesterday. Sladovok. What happened about that ?"

" Oh, that is under control, but it can wait for the time being. Two major arrests in one day is enough to be going on with, surely ? What time is it now ?"

" Two-thirty."

" We shall have to hurry, the match starts at three."

" Are we arresting him before or after the game ?"

" Before. In the dressing-room with his trousers down."

They drove through the football traffic to Craven Cottage, parked right outside the ground, identifying themselves to traffic police, and introduced themselves to the Fulham officials.

" I need to speak to the Blackpool manager," said Glass. " But don't tell him who it is. I do not want to arouse any suspicions at this stage. Just say there is a call for him in the office." The policemen were escorted to the secretary's office. " I hope Blackpool have brought along a good substitute," whispered Glass to Moon. " O'Malley has scored five goals in the last six games."

The Blackpool manager arrived and Glass explained the situation. He looked grave. " I don't believe it," he said. " Are you sure you have the right man?"

" I'd stake my reputation on it," said Glass, " which is considerable."

The manager shook his head. " He is the only player involved I take it? Such a thing reflects badly on the club."

" Positive," Glass assured him. He looked at his chronometer. " It is quarter to already. We had better go down. I'm sorry it has to be before the game."

They walked down to the dressing-rooms. A smell of wintergreen pervaded the air.

" That one is ours at the end. I had better tell the sub he is playing."

" We'll go in first," said Glass. " Are you ready?" Moon nodded. They marched forward and Glass flung open the door.

The dressing-room was empty.

" Christ, we are too late. They've gone onto the field."

" What will we do now?"

" There is only one thing to do. I'll have to go out after him."

" But he will see you coming."

" No he won't. Which is the referee's changing-room?"

The Blackpool manager pointed. " In there with the linesmen." Glass strode straight in.

" Surely he can't be going to stop the game. There are over fifteen thousand spectators out there. We'd have a riot on our hands."

Moon agreed. They waited impatiently. The home team filed out of their dressing-room and clattered down the stone-floored corridor to the tunnel.

" Five to three," said Moon. " Five minutes to kick off."

The Blackpool manager paced up and down.

At two minutes to three, the changing-room door opened and out trotted the two linesmen, followed by the portly figure of the referee in his all black strip. Moon peered with horror at the familiar gnarled face.

" Good God," he ejaculated in a rare moment of blasphemy.

" Don't get too excited, son," murmured the ' referee '. " Just stay in sight." And taking the white match ball in his hands, Detective Chief Inspector Walter Glass of Scotland Yard ran out onto the Craven Cottage pitch to the traditional abuse of the English soccer crowd.

The linesmen took up their positions on either side of the field as Glass blew his whistle to bring the two captains to the centre spot.

From the touchline, Sergeant Moon watched as the men shook hands and the toss was made. The Fulham captain won and elected for the sides to change ends. The players lined up for the kick-off. Brendan O'Malley took his place at the centre of the Blackpool forwards. Still holding the match ball, Glass walked over to him. Behind the ball were the handcuffs.

" All right, ref?" greeted the player.

The " referee " flung down the ball. " Brendan O'Malley, I arrest you for the murder of Michael Spencer." The handcuffs snapped round the footballer's wrist. O'Malley struggled, but Glass was a big man and held firm. " You are not obliged to say anything, but I must warn you that anything you do say will be taken down and may be used in evidence. Now just keep walking to that tunnel, son, or I'll break your arm. No use trying to get away. There are over a hundred police on this ground." Glass wondered what they were making of it all. The crowd cheered, puzzled but delighted that the opposition centre forward should be escorted off the pitch before the game had even begun. The rest of the players watched in amazement as the bogus referee and his charge walked unswervingly past them. Glass ignored the comments. Moon stepped forward to help him as they reached the touchline and the real referee and the Blackpool substitute ran out onto the field.

" We'll have him in the dressing-room I think," said Glass. " Go and radio to the Yard for a van."

Glass dragged O'Malley into the Blackpool dressing-room. The players' clothes hung on pegs around the walls, linament and bandages covered the floor and a few personal articles were laid on the wooden slatted bench. Glass took off the handcuffs but, before his prisoner could strike him, butted him with his forehead, knocking him down onto the bench.

" You are resisting arrest," warned the Chief Inspector, menacingly. He brought his right arm back and thudded his fist against the other's mouth; loosening four teeth.

The door opened the Sergeant Moon rushed in. " Don't hit him again, sir."

" Why not?" Glass's fist smashed into O'Malley's jaw

and blood ran down the Inspector's wrist. Moon winced. "Why not?" repeated Glass. "This is the man that killed a copper. O'Malley was barely conscious. "Give him something to think about while he is watching colour TV in his cell." A left hook crashed into O'Malley's eye. "See if his Yogi Bear mask will fit him now." The eye closed. "Now listen, I want to know where Patsy is hiding. If you don't tell me now I will hit you until you do, and you can get brain damage from too many blows to the head."

Moon rushed in to hold back Glass's hovering fist. "At least wait until he comes round before asking him," he protested.

"He is awake all right, aren't you, O'Malley?"

The erstwhile centre forward groaned and looked helplessly at Moon through his good eye.

Suddenly, the dressing-room door opened.

"Whatever is going on? The Inquisition?"

"What the hell are you doing here?" Glass asked Timothy Slade.

The reporter sat on the bench opposite the prisoner. "Deduction. Sue told me about the football tie-in. Word came into the office about the post-office job in Fulham. I checked the fixtures, put two and two together and here I am. I saw the arrest from the Press Box. Very theatrical. The sports hacks up there couldn't believe it." His face hardened as he looked across at the prisoner. "I take it this is one of them."

"Brendan O'Malley, footballer, thief and murderer."

"I never killed no one." The words came with difficulty through the torn lips. "That was Patsy. It was all his idea."

"Family loyalty," commented Glass. "Where is Patsy now?"

"Hiding out before we go back on the coach tonight."

" So you've got him on the coach now? What is he? Substitute goalkeeper?"

" Where is he hiding?" This time it was Slade who spoke.

" At a house in the East End." He choked out an address. " He's got a gun." More blood trickled out of his mouth. " Get me a doctor for Christ's sake."

Glass leaned forward and looked the man in the eye. " You can wait for your doctor, O'Malley, and while you are waiting, think of a little girl without a hand, and if you bleed to death before the ambulance comes that will be your bad luck."

Moon thrust a towel at the Chief Inspector. " To mop up the mess," he explained. " Hadn't we better put his clothes on?"

" Which peg is yours?" The prisoner pointed, and Glass fetched over his shirt and trousers. " Get these on." He took out his handcuffs again and looked round. " Where's Slade?"

" He went out a couple of minutes ago, sir."

" Oh Christ, no." Glass ran to the door, the handcuffs dangling at his wrist. He turned to Moon agitatedly. " He's locked us in."

" I don't understand."

" The key must have been at the other side of the door. And he has got Kelly's address."

" But why?"

" Because, Sergeant Moon, Timothy Slade wanted to get Patsy Kelly before us and if he does Patsy Kelly is a dead man. Timothy Slade is The Executioner."

It was one of the ground stewards who unlocked the Blackpool dressing-room door, but, by the time Glass reached the car to radio Scotland Yard, eight minutes had elapsed.

"I want Detective Chief Inspector Knox," he told the switchboard, and hoped he was in the office on a Saturday afternoon. He was lucky. Robin Knox came on the line, and Glass told him briefly what had happened. "He has gone to a house in Whitechapel," he said, giving him the address. "Get hold of some men and meet us outside. And hurry. If we don't get there in time, not only will Kelly be with the angels but Slade will be away. You can bet your life that he has organised his escape route as efficiently as his executions."

"How did you get on to Slade?" asked Moon as they speeded out of Fulham towards King's Road. Brendon O'Malley had been taken to the nearest hospital by ambulance with a police escort. Fulham were beating the re-organised Blackpool team, one-nil. Glass had changed out of his referee's kit.

"A pure long-shot," admitted Glass. "Sue was telling me about Timothy Slade's background, illegitimate son of a peer, and my mind went back to the Debbings crime. As the Highlys had no children, it was assumed that there was nobody with a strong personal motive for vegence."

"Except Lady Highly."

"I could not visualise a seventy-odd-year-old titled lady stringing up a burglar in one of London's parks at the dead of night, Sergeant."

"She could have hired someone."

"Kindly listen to my story. You might learn something. As I was saying, the Highlys had no children. But after listening to Sue, it occurred to me that if Lord Highly had fathered an illegitimate child, then here would be the number one suspect."

"But you had no idea the child would be Slade?"

165

" None at all. It was only when I heard that the mother's name was Sladovok that I began to wonder. The age was about right and Slade is as good an Anglicism as any for Sladovok. So I checked *The Megaphone* personnel files, and what do I find? Timothy Slade's real name is Timon Sladovok. He had not bothered to officially change it by deed poll. His insurance card still carried the original Polish name."

" But that does not prove he is The Executioner."

" No. But it was a good start. Then came Trevellyn's murder. Slade was with me at the Old Bailey trial and you heard his strong views that day on capital punishment."

" Roughly the same as yours, weren't they, sir?"

Glass ignored the remark. " And finally, the Post Office murders. Slade has been following this case from the start and has kept with it when the other papers have left it to the agencies. Obviously, all the time he was waiting for a clue which would reveal the identity of the villains to him so that he could get at them before us. Remember the last Executioner letter? ' I am going after a murderer the police have been unable to trace '."

" I wonder why Chief Inspector Knox did not think of all this?"

" Spends too much time reading books," said Glass unkindly. " Destroys your brain in the end, you know. He should be like me, get out to places like the Arfricaana Club and the Establishment. They'd teach him a thing or two. You can't beat experience. Mind you, he'll be in at the kill, so no doubt he will collect a lot of the credit going. He won't miss an opportunity like that."

" But it was you who tipped him off."

Glass looked sheepish. " Yes, well, he's not a bad lad. Sue seems to like him."

"Oh." Moon wondered why Sue's opinion should be of such relevance. "She's played a big part in this, one way and another, this Sue."

"Yes, I suppose she has," agreed Glass non-commitally.

He lurched the car sideways and missed a double-decker bus by millimetres. Moon gulped and swallowed his Polo mint. Glass drove on, as if auditioning for an Evil Knievel film. The siren on the car opened up a gap in the traffic as they roared along Victoria Embankment at sixty-five. Moon shut his eyes. They shot through two sets of red traffic lights and were still doing over fifty when they passed the Tower.

"Nearly there," said Glass calmly as they came into Whitechapel. Moon was not familiar with the district, but Glass seemed to know all of London like a seasoned taxi-driver and found the house without any trouble.

Another police car, bearing Robin Knox, drew up simultaneously.

"There is no car outside," said Glass. "We are either too early or too late." He opened the car door. "And there is only one way to find out. Let's go."

TWENTY-FOUR

It was a typical East End, two-up-two-down, due-for-demolition, terraced house.

Patsy Kelly sat in the downstairs back room. In modern parlance it would have been called a kitchen-dinette, but throughout its eighty-year history it had only ever been referred to as a scullery. The house belonged to a friend of his who was currently enjoying a vacation in one of Her Majesty's Prisons.

A chipped slopstone, ancient gas water heater and equally ancient gas oven indicated the kitchen portion. The "dinette" comprised an oak table, two painted kitchen chairs and a sofa, all there was room for. A dull coke fire burned in the grate of a black-leaded bungalow range which would have been worth a fortune in more trendy surroundings. A worn black mat covered the brown oilcloth in front of the kerb.

Patsy Kelly sat on the sofa counting bundles of paper money overflowing from four hold-alls. On the floor by his feet lay two children's masks—Yogi Bear and Barney Flintstone.

It was twenty-past three. Kelly leaned down and switched on an old electric radio standing by the skirting board, dust covering its walnut cabinet. He turned the big needle to the sports programme on Radio Two, or the Light Programme as it was inscribed on the dial.

He had arranged to meet his step-brother at five-thirty outside Craven Cottage. Brendan had again been able to fix him a seat on the team coach back to Blackpool. He had been staying at Brendan's flat since the police had discovered his Liverpool address, but now he was contemplating moving to London permanently. Blackpool was a dangerous place for him now that he was a wanted man. He dare not go out on the streets. Too many people knew him. In London, he was unknown.

The doorbell rang.

He froze. It rang again. Who would know he was here? Except Brendan.

"Patsy. Are you there?" Brendan's voice. He should

have been on the field. What had gone wrong? Throwing the money aside, Patsy jumped to his feet and ran to the door. He pulled back the Yale catch and started to open it. An insistent foot pushed it the rest of the way.

"Hello, Patsy," smiled the well-dressed stranger. "I do impersonations."

"Wha . . ." began Kelly, but he got no further. Before he could push the door to a foot landed squarely in his groin. He emitted a falsetto scream of pure agony before falling unconscious on the floor.

Timothy Slade wasted no time. He stepped into the hall, shut the door after him and leant over Kelly's prostrate body. From his pocket he took a length of rope which he tied round his victim's neck.

"This is for Carol Spencer whose husband you killed. And for Gail Hutchinson whose hand you shot off." He pulled the rope tight. "I have not got the time to do this the way I would like. Slowly. Say your prayers my friend," and with a swift tug he jerked the rope to break Kelly's neck. As a last gesture, he took from his pocket one of the familiar small cards bearing the sign of the gallows and stuck it into Patsy Kelly's half-open mouth.

He had not been in the house more than sixty seconds, but he knew they would be after him now. He had kept the engine of the Audi running. He ran down the path and jumped into the driving-seat. With a squeal of tyres the car roared off up the road.

"Did you get what you wanted?"

The Executioner turned to his passenger. "I did." And with one arm around Sue Owen he drove off into the sunset.

TWENTY-FIVE

Detective Chief Inspector Knox was the first man to reach the house. He banged hard on the door with his fists. Glass, puffing slightly behind him, knelt on the ground and squinted through the letter box.

"He's on the floor. We'll have to break the door down."

"It is only a Yale lock. Easy enough." Knox stood back and aimed a high kick, level with the lock. The door flew open as the wood holding the catch splintered.

"Evans," shouted Knox.

"Yes, sir."

"We're too late, but radio for an ambulance anyway." He removed the card from Kelly's mouth. "It was The Executioner all right."

"We must have him picked up. Sergeant!" he called. Moon came running across. "Put out a call for an orange Audi 100GL, R registration. Slade must be apprehended tonight. I want a watch on all airports and seaports."

"Excuse me, sir." Sergeant Evans approached leading a stout man with braces holding up his ballooning trousers and wearing a button-up woollen vest. "This is the gentleman from next door. Says he saw Slade coming in."

"Don't know about coming in, but I heard him going out. What's going on in 'ere. Disturbing a bloke's Saturday kip." He looked down at the dead man. "Stone me. What happened to 'im?"

"You say someone entered this house a few minutes

ago?" barked Knox.

"Yeah, young bloke he was. Smart. He was in a posh car, bright orange, one of them foreign jobs."

"An Audi?"

"Might have been. Here, did he do that?"

"Seems like it."

"Stone me. I'm glad he never came to my house."

"He wasn't looking for you. How long is it since he left?"

"Just before you lot came. I'm surprised you didn't see him."

"Christ, just too late," said Glass.

"He had a bit of stuff with him. Nice-looking piece she was."

"What!" cried Knox and Glass simultaneously.

"Waiting in the car. Only young."

"Sue," said Knox. "I'm going after her."

Glass pulled him back by the arm. "Hang on, lad. The patrols are looking for him."

"You don't understand. That's my girl he's got in there. He'll kill her."

"I don't think Slade will harm Sue," said Glass.

"I can't risk it. I love her."

"So do I," said Glass quietly.

Knox looked at him in amazement. "You?"

"Yes," replied Glass. "Sue Owen is my daughter."

TWENTY-SIX

"Where are we going now?" asked Sue as they sped out of Whitechapel in the Audi.

"Back to the City."

"And then?"

"And then, you are going home and I am going away."

"Away? Where to?"

"I haven't decided."

She looked at him closely. "Is something wrong? I thought I heard a scream in that house."

Slade negotiated a roundabout at breakneck speed.

"Chief Inspector Glass was asking me about you," she said slowly. "And about your father. Something to do with this Executioner business. You haven't anything to do with that, Tim, have you?"

Slade laughed. "A perceptive man our friend Mr. Glass."

"What do you mean?"

"And he has the right ideas too. But he is not so keen to put them into practice. Very indignant he was when Trevellyn only got seven years, but he didn't try to do anything about it."

"And you did, is that what you are saying?"

"Yes, Sue. I killed Trevellyn."

"You are joking?" She instinctively reached for the door handle but Slade pulled her back with his left arm. "Don't get alarmed," he said. "I am not going to hurt you. I am not a mad killer, you know."

"You are The Executioner."

"Yes. But the only people I have killed are murderers who deserved to die."

"You killed the man in St. James's Park as well?"

"That man, Sue, killed my father. For no reason. I reckon that that killing was justified."

"What about the others?"

"One other. So far that is. Yes, I think they were justified. I went to see the old lady whose husband was battered to death by Trevellyn. Her spirit had gone. She had lost everything. One pathetic old man, not well off, not very important perhaps, but she loved him. And the beast that killed him is set free in five years, maybe to kill someone else. I am proud that I killed Trevellyn. He did not deserve to live."

"You sound like a crusader."

"Not a bad description. Why do you think I chose this way of drawing attention to the state of law and order? Because it seemed the most effective, and who can dispute that now?"

"But did you have to kill? Surely a petition on its own . . ."

"No impact. This was the only way."

"They will say you are insane."

"That is a matter of opinion. Society is constantly changing its views on madness according to contemporary ideas."

"And now they are after you?"

"I am afraid so. They have guessed who The Executioner is. Or rather your father has. Oh yes, I know a few things about your family history too. I am an investigative reporter, you know, or so *The Megaphone* advertised me. I know about Glass's divorce when you were a little girl. Your

173

mother married again, a chap named Bobby Owen, and your name was changed by deed poll."

A police car passed by in the opposite direction, blue light flashing.

"What are you going to do with me?"

"Don't look worried. I am not going to hurt you. For a start I will get away better on my own. I have my plans made, you know. Besides, I like you, Sue, and I like your father."

"What are you going to do? Where will you go?"

"That I had better not tell you, but I would say they are not far behind me. I must drop you off soon. A bright orange Audi is not the most difficult car to spot." He pulled in to the kerb and opened the passenger door. "Good luck, Sue. Thanks for the good times. Don't think too badly of me and give my regards to Detective Chief Inspector Knox. I hope you will be happy with him."

"How . . .?" she began, but he held up his hand to silence her.

"I know everything," smiled The Executioner as he closed the car door and accelerated away leaving her standing speechless outside Lloyds in Leadenhall Street.

He only drove another half mile. As he came into Cheapside towards the Cathedral, he slowed down, switched off the engine and coasted to a halt on the double yellow lines. Taking his brief-case from the car, he calmly stepped out into the traffic, crossed the road and joined the throng of pedestrians on the opposite pavement. By the time the angry hooting of horns drew attention to the orange Audi, he was on the escalator descending into St. Paul's underground station.

The train was already in the platform, bound for Ealing Broadway, but Slade's journey would not be extending that far. He chose the front carriage and sat next to an off-duty guard.

" Got the right time, mate ?"

" Quarter-past four," replied Slade. The match at Craven Cottage would still be in progress. He alighted at Marble Arch and emerged into the open air at the exit beside the Cumberland Hotel opposite Hyde Park. He crossed Oxford Street and waited in a doorway for a No. 30 bus. The earlier sun was now obscured by clouds and, although lighting-up time was not until six o'clock, most vehicles were already using their side-lights.

He kept a careful watch for policemen. By now his description would have been circulated, and he was already well known to many men on the Force by virtue of his job as a crime reporter. A job he would never be able to return to.

At last the bus came. Slade took the front seat on the upper deck, the best vantage point. It lumbered along Park Lane, turned right at Hyde Park Corner into Knightsbridge and forked left at Brompton Road past Harrods. Towards Fulham.

The Executioner had one more score to settle. Brendan O'Malley was somewhere in a Fulham hospital recovering from his beating at the hands of Detective Chief Inspector Glass. To Slade, a beating was not enough.

Brendan O'Malley would be having a visit from The Executioner.

TWENTY-SEVEN

The Scotland Yard men were still at Whitechapel when word came in about the abandoned Audi.

" Either he had another vehicle lined up or he is taking a chance on not being recognised on public transport," said Glass.

" I wonder where he is making for," said Moon.

" More to the point : what has he done with Sue?" Robin Knox looked haggard.

" I shouldn't worry, sir," said Evans, soothingly. " He has no reason to harm her."

His optimism was justified a minute later when Scotland Yard radioed through to say that Sue Owen was in a phone kiosk asking for Detective Chief Inspector Glass. Glass spoke to the switchboard. " She is outside the Royal Exchange," he told the others when he had finished. " You and Sergeant Evans might as well come in our car, Robin, and let your men take yours back to the Yard."

" Shall I lock up the house?" asked Sergeant Evans. The ambulance had taken Patsy Kelly to the mortuary and the stolen money and masks had been replaced in the hold-alls and lay safely in the boot of Glass's car.

" Hurry then." Evans was back in seconds, and they set off for the City.

" Sue said that Slade intended to abandon the car."

" Which he did do, two streets further on."

" Right. So he could be anywhere now."

" At least he won't get out of the country so easily."

" Unless he has a false passport," pointed out Evans, pessimistically.

" Either way, it looks like the end of The Executioner," said Knox.

" Why do you say that?"

" Well, it has got to be, hasn't it? We know who he is now."

" But if we can't find him," argued Glass, " it will make no difference."

" So you think he will carry on his campaign?"

" It is possible."

" After all," broke in Sergeant Evans, " he hasn't finished this job yet."

" What do you mean?"

" Well, he might have done for Kelly, but O'Malley is still unharmed." Moon looked Heavenward at the last remark and coughed nervously in Glass's direction. The car gave a sudden jolt as Glass slammed on the brakes.

" Of course, that's it," he cried, turning round in his seat and ignoring the gesticulations of the driver alongside him who had been forced to swerve halfway across the road. " That is where he will go. Which hospital was O'Malley taken to?"

" I think it was St. Stephen's in Fulham Road," said Moon. " Either that or the Fulham Hospital in St. Dunstan's Road."

" We'll try St. Stephen's first." They moved forward again.

" I can't see him doing it," said Knox. " Think of the risk he'd be taking and to what avail? He has proved his point."

" He likes to fulfil his predictions though. Like

Muhammed Ali. We'll pick up Sue, then get down to St. Stephen's."

Sue was at the Royal Exchange in Leadenhall Street, shivering in her light denim jacket. Knox ushered her in the back seat with obvious relief and introduced her to Sergeant Evans.

"Quite a family gathering," remarked the Sergeant as they set off for Fulham. "Join London's most exclusive crime fighting squad."

At St. Stephen's Hospital, Glass spoke to the doctor in charge of Casualty.

"Someone rang up ten minutes ago to ask if O'Malley had been brought here," said the houseman. "He did not give his name."

"It must be Slade," said Glass. "We are on the right track but we have not got much time. Where is O'Malley now?"

"In a private room. He has had an operation to set his broken jaw. It is all wired up. Someone gave him a right going over."

"Terrible," said Glass, shaking his head as if he did not know what the world was coming to. "Can I see him?"

"He is covered in bandages and cannot talk."

"Perfect," said Glass. He explained briefly to the doctor what he wanted. "I am expecting an attempt on this man's life. I want to take his place in that room, wrapped up in bandages. When the assailant comes in, he will find me instead of O'Malley. When he attacks I shall arrest him."

"What if he is armed?"

"I don't think he will be. His usual method is the rope. Strangulation."

"I see."

"Can you take us to him now?" He turned to Knox.

178

"Is Sue in the car?"

"Yes. With Sergeant Evans."

"Good. Now then, I want you and Moon to come with me. We shall have to find somewhere for you to hide, ready in case anything goes wrong."

There were three rooms in the small private wing, all leading off the one narrow corridor. O'Malley was in the second.

"We can move him into the end one," offered the doctor. "You take his place in the middle and perhaps your men would care to secrete themselves in the first. If you need help you only need to shout; the walls are paper thin."

"Sounds O.K." Glass was given pyjamas and his face was bandaged by a student nurse of Indian extraction. A porter brought a trolley and wheeled O'Malley into the empty room at the end where a nurse made up his bed. Glass took his place beneath the sheets in the middle room. Slits in the bandages enabled him to see, but he himself was unrecognisable. Moon thought he looked like a refugee from the British Museum's Tutankhamen Exhibition.

"All set?" Glass's muffled voice came through the bandages. Moon and Knox wished him well and retreated to the next room. The houseman returned to Casualty. Glass lay on the bed, hot beneath the binding, waiting for The Executioner.

Blackpool eventually beat Fulham by three goals to one, the last two goals being scored, ironically, by their substitute, "Ginger" Blundell. The home supporters were incensed with this outcome and showed their disapproval by throwing bricks through the windows of the visitor's coach.

Understandably, the Blackpool contingent did not take

kindly to this and retaliated by attacking the London fans with every sharp and blunt instrument they could lay their hands on.

The resultant carnage from this fracas was deposited at the Casualty Department of St. Stephen's Hospital in Fulham which took on the appearance of Crimea at the height of the battle.

Timothy Slade experienced no difficulty in entering the building unnoticed among the walking wounded, and the acquisition of a white coat from an unlocked cupboard ensured his further invisibility. He left his briefcase under a pile of linen and set about finding his quarry.

Fortune favoured the killer. He stopped a nurse in the corridor leading to the wards, and it transpired that she had been on duty earlier in O'Malley's room. Slade explained that he was new to the hospital, so the nurse, who had been brought up on Mills and Boon and had a yearning for young, eligible doctors, walked with him to the private wing and pointed out the door. The " doctor " thanked her, squeezed her hand and watched her skip coyly down the corridor, giggling most of the way.

Then he took out his knife.

He knew he would not have time here for elaborate hangings. Justice would come swiftly to Brendan O'Malley. He looked carefully around him. Nobody was about. He had no idea that Detective Chief Inspector Glass was lying not ten feet away, swathed in bandages, waiting for him.

Silently he opened the door. There on the bed lay the bandaged figure. As Slade moved in he started to rise, but The Executioner was too fast. He strode across the room and plunged the blade deep into the heart of the man he thought was Brenden O'Malley.

TWENTY-EIGHT

Tuesday, March 23rd

Without exception, the morning papers carried the "Executioner Affair" as their lead story. EXECUTIONER KEEPS APPOINTMENT blazoned the *Mail* across its front page. P.O. BANDITS FALL TO EXECUTIONER hailed the *Express*. *The Times* was more circumspect: EXECUTIONER CLAIMS MORE VICTIMS IN WEST LONDON. *The Megaphone* audaciously turned to its advantage the fact that its own crime reporter WAS The Executioner and ran a banner headline proclaiming OUR MAN AT THE GALLOWS.

EXECUTIONER ESCAPES DRAGNET headed a *Telegraph* story which described how, whilst The Executioner was quietly murdering his victim, a senior Scotland Yard detective was in the room next door wrapped in bandages, waiting to arrest him.

"He went into the wrong room by mistake," Glass told the Assistant Commissioner.

"The right room from his point of view."

Glass ignored him. "The nurse who directed him was the one nurse in the hospital who knew that O'Malley had been moved. It was she, in fact, who made up his new bed."

"Otherwise, you would have been dead now." The Assistant Commissioner spoke in a voice which suggested that the loss would not have distressed him overmuch.

"Poetic justice I suppose," sighed Glass.

"So what is your next move?"

"All the exits are sealed, sir. He has to be in the country somewhere."

"Then I can take it," said the Assistant Commissioner heavily, "that you will find him, you and Detective Chief Inspector Knox between you. And soon."

"I did catch the Post Office boys," reminded Glass.

"Yes. But you didn't hold on to them very well, did you? One strangled and the other stabbed, in one case whilst the police were next door and in the other after the police had kindly supplied directions."

"Put like that, sir . . ."

"I will say no more, Chief Inspector, other than the newspapers have made us out to be dunderheads. It is up to you to change that opinion. Good day to you Chief Inspector."

Timothy Slade, sometimes known as The Executioner, spent the night in a small hotel in Craven Road, in Bayswater. His departure from St. Stephen's Hospital had been effected without incident. Retrieving his briefcase from the linen cupboard in exchange for the white coat, he had merely walked unchallenged from the building, unseen by Sergeant Evans and Sue Owen in the police car parked round the corner, and onto the bus with the same aplomb he had shown when departing from Wormwood Scrubs after murdering Robert Trevellyn.

He stayed in his room all evening and compiled two letters.

His first act on rising was to make some changes in his appearance. With a sharp pair of scissors, he cut off all his hair to crew-cut length. He hooked a pair of plain glass, horn-rimmed spectacles over his now protruding ears and removed his dental plate bearing one molar.

The substitution of sneakers for his platform shoes took inches off his height, and instead of his customary smart suit he donned a pair of denim jeans, polo-necked sweater and plastic bomber jacket with a picture of Elvis Presley on the back. He put all his old clothes in the briefcase, which he placed out of sight on top of the wardrobe, and set off for Euston without his breakfast, posting the letters on the way.

He caught the Circle Line tube from Paddington to Euston Square and walked the few hundred yards along Euston Road to the main line station. Nobody gave him a second glance as he bought his ticket and boarded the same 7.45 train that Glass and Moon had caught twelve days before.

There was nothing on his person to connect him with Timothy Slade. The driving licence he carried bore the name Steve Day, as did the AA membership card and the cheque book.

Prompt on time, the Inter-City express pulled out of the platform bound for Glasgow. But The Executioner was not travelling all the way.

TWENTY-NINE

Wednesday, March 24th

Thanks to the super-efficiency of the first-class post, Slade's letter to *The Times* arrived at that newspaper's offices some five hours after he posted it and it was subsequently published the next morning.

Dear Sir,

My promise has been kept, albeit at the expense of my anonymity, and two more criminals who should have been hanged have been punished according to the law of The Executioner.

This shall be my last sentence. I value my own freedom and, besides, my point has been made and not made in vain.

The response from the public in the form of letters, petitions and campaigns to bring back the death penalty shows that the silent majority are silent no longer and it is inevitable that the Government must at last accede to the wishes of the electorate.

I thank those who have supported my campaign and urge them to continue the fight to make our country once again a safe place to live in.

TIMOTHY SLADE (alias The Executioner).

" What do you think of it?" asked Detective Chief Inspector Knox. He had arrived at Glass's flat with Sergeant Evans shortly after breakfast to discuss plans for apprehending The Executioner. Sergeant Moon was already there, having travelled from Golder's Green on the back of Ethel's 250 c.c. motor cycle.

" I think we should leave it at that," said Glass. " He has obviously no intention of continuing with the killings."

The doorbell rang and he went to answer it.

" Hello, love, come in and join the party." Sue Owen stepped into the room.

" I've got the day off so I thought I'd come round and

find out what has happened." She smiled across at Robin Knox.

" We've just been talking about Tim's latest letter," said Glass. " Have you seen it?"

" No, but let me go and make a cup of tea, then you can show it to me."

" He is still a murderer at large," continued Knox as Sue went into the kitchen. " We can't just let him go."

" Why not? We have enough other jobs that need seeing to. There is the forgery at the Royal Academy, the Barclays Bank job at Charing Cross, that computer theft yesterday at . . ."

" Yes I know, but . . ."

" Odd how there have been no violent jobs in the last fortnight," mused Glass shamelessly. " Since the first Executioner letter."

" There was a murder in Clapham on Sunday."

" Yes, but that was a girl who found her girl friend with another woman." He rubbed his chin ruminatively. " We never used to get crimes like that in the old days. I don't understand these modern ways. I blame all these magazines like *Cosmopolitan*. Gives women funny ideas."

" You are right there," agreed Sergeant Evans. " I will only allow Mrs. Evans to read the *Woman's Weekly*."

Sue brought in the cups and saucers. " Let me help you," said Evans, and he followed her into the kitchen.

Knox persisted. " I still think we ought to arrest him. This whole thing could quite easily have led to anarchy. And still might."

" Drastic measures sometimes have to be taken to jolt people out of their complacency," said Glass. " All the men he killed should have been hanged anyway."

" I'll agree with that. In fact, I would stay that there are

185

very few policemen who would not like to see the death penalty restored. But the point remains that by taking the law into his own hands Slade could have incited half the country to riot."

"We won't argue," said Glass. "Not if you want permission to marry my daughter."

"Permission!" cried Sue, reappearing with a plate of scones. "That went out with The Beatles."

"More modern ideas," grumbled Glass.

Sergeant Evans carried in a steaming teapot. "Anyone take sugar?" he enquired.

"Funny how you can tell a married man by the way he sets a table," approved Knox. "I am surprised you didn't bring your apron, Sergeant."

Sergeant Moon crouched in a corner stroking a tiny grey and white kitten. Glass lit up a Craven A to go with his tea, and offered the packet round the room. Nobody took one. The kitten wriggled free from Moon's fondling and ran over to Sue who poured it some milk in her saucer.

"I see Sailor is making himself at home," she said.

"I haven't mentioned it to the landlady yet," said Glass. "This will set relations back another ten years. I'll never get the garage roof mended now. She's a vindictive sod is Mrs. Cowan. Doesn't approve of pets in the house."

"These are the nicest scones I've tasted in years," complimented Knox.

"Sue made them," said Glass. "I've told her she ought to move in and look after me like a dutiful daughter."

"She is moving in with me like a dutiful wife."

"Have you set the date yet?" enquired Sergeant Evans.

"Listen to him. Can't wait to get everyone in the same boat as himself."

"Whit-Monday," said Sue, firmly.

"About time you were getting married, Sergeant Moon," said Glass. "How long have you and Ethel been engaged?"

"Five years, sir, but my Ethel likes time to make decisions."

"If she takes much longer, you'll be paying for the bouquets out of your pension."

"So we are leaving the case then," said Knox. "The Commisioner won't like it."

"I had a letter from Slade myself," said Glass.

"You never told me."

"It only came this morning. You didn't give me time."

"What did it say?"

"Nothing much. The same as in *The Times*. He has finished his campaign and retired to obscurity. And he enclosed a cheque for five hundred pounds."

"Whatever for?"

"For me to give to P.C. Spencer's widow. Thought it might be dangerous for him to deliver it himself, her being a bobby's wife."

"That's funny," said Sergeant Evans.

"How do you mean, funny?"

"Well, I heard a story going round that Slade, or somebody, had given five hundred to the old lady whose husband was killed by Trevellyn."

"You never told me this, Sergeant," reproved Knox.

"It was only a rumour, sir. Someone mentioned it in the canteen last night. To tell you the truth, I'd forgotten."

"I wonder if it was Slade. He earned good money at *The Megaphone*. He isn't short of a few bob. But why?"

"He once told me he wished he could do something for the victims," said Sue. "It was when we were coming back from Carlisle."

Knox jumped to his feet, spilling his teacup over Glass's

carpet and swallowing a mouthful of tea. "That's it," he spluttered. "That is where we will find Slade. Carlisle. Don't you see? He will go to the Hutchinsons with their five hundred pounds."

Glass looked doubtful. "It is possible, I suppose."

"Come on, we are going after him."

"He could have just posted it."

"He had to get out of London, didn't he? I bet he is hiding up in Cumbria."

"You make him sound like quarry to be hunted," said Sue.

"So he is. Are we going?"

"I suppose so," conceded Glass.

They journeyed in Knox's duty car, a Cortina 2000. The Chief Inspector drove with Sue alongside him. She had insisted on joining them.

"I fancy something to eat," said Glass when they joined the M1.

"I know a place," said Knox. He took the exit a mile before the services at Newport Pagnall and drove into the village past the Aston Martin works.

"It is a country pub that serves home-made grub." Sue remembered her last trip up the motorway to Carlisle with Tim when they ate at the service station and concluded that Robin Knox had more style. All the same, she did not like the idea of her one-time friend being apprehended, a feeling shared by her father.

"He's had plenty of time to get to the Hutchinsons and disappear again," he whispered as they ate their Huntingdon Pie baked in cider at The Dolphin. "So don't worry."

They reached Carlisle in five and a half hours. Sergeant Moon was stiff from the journey, crushed in the back between Sergeant Evans and Glass, both men of considerable girth. Knox drove out to the Hutchinson's cottage on Glass's directions, through the country lanes into the hills.

The family were having tea. The log fire burned away in the living-room and a new budgie chattered in its cage. Jean Hutchinson had cooked chicken pie with mushrooms, onions and fried potatoes. Glass noticed that little Gail ate with one hand and that her stump was pushed into the sleeve of her cardigan, and at that moment he was glad to think of Patsy Kelly's demise.

"Yes, he did come," admitted Mrs. Hutchinson, in answer to Knox's question. "He came yesterday and left us five hundred pounds for Gail."

"Did he say where he was going?"

"No."

"Did he look any different from when you last saw him?"

She hesitated. Her husband answered for her.

"Look, Chief Inspector. We know all about this bloke and what he has done and, as far as we are concerned, we are bloody glad that he did it. If the Law had his attitude then my little girl would not have lost her hand. Timothy Slade has done my family a good turn, and I am not talking about the money. He did not have to give us that. He is a good bloke and there is no way that anyone here is going to help you put him away. Do I make myself clear? No disrespect, but I would rather go to jail myself first."

The speech shattered everyone in the room. Glass was the first to speak.

"Put the money through the letter-box, did he?" he said carefully. "Well, if none of you saw him, Mr. Hutchinson, then there is nothing more we can do here." His steel hard stare froze Knox's objections before they were voiced.

"Would you like a cup of tea while you are here?"

asked Jean Hutchinson, trying to relieve the tension.

Glass took out his packet of Craven A and put it on the mantelpiece while he searched in his greatcoat pockets for his matches.

" No thanks. We have two policemen and a young lady waiting in the car," he said. " They will be getting impatient. Thanks all the same and sorry to have intruded." He ushered Knox off the premises.

" Just too late," he said when they got outside. " A good idea of yours but, just too late. Back to London, then, eh?" Knox nodded. He knew when he was beaten. He climbed wearily into the driving-seat.

" Hell," cursed Glass. " I've left my cigarettes in the house. I shan't be a minute." He ran back and opened the door without knocking.

A man was coming out of the kitchen. He stopped dead when he saw Glass. Nobody in the room moved.

He was a young man with a crew cut and horn-rimmed spectacles. He wore a polo-necked sweater and denim jeans. Nobody spoke.

" I left my cigarettes," said the Chief Inspector, going over to the mantelpiece and picking up the red packet.

" This is Peter Otto, our new farmhand," said Dick Hutchinson at last. Lamely.

The family watched and waited.

Glass looked unwaveringly into the unmistakable brown eyes of Timothy Slade. " Pleased to meet you, Mr. Otto," he said. He found his matches and lit a Craven A. " I hope you will be very happy here." A tear formed in Slade's eye and his face filled with gratitude. " We won't disturb you again," said the detective and, closing the door of the cottage, he walked back to the car.